COUSINS

by
Meto Jovanovski

Translated by
Sylvia Wallace Holton
and
Meto Jovanovski

Mercury House, Incorporated
San Francisco

Acknowledgments

A literal translation by Zhivka Stockdale of this novel was used as a working text for the present translation.

The Faculty Senate of the University of the District of Columbia generously supported the project with a Research Award in the summer of 1982. This award enabled Sylvia Holton to visit the region in which the novel is set and to work with Meto Jovanovski recasting, editing, and perfecting the translation.

Originally published as *Budaletinki.*
English translation ©1987 by Sylvia Holton and Meto Jovanovski

Published in the United States by
Mercury House
300 Montgomery Street
San Francisco, California

Distributed to the trade by
Kampmann & Company, Inc.
New York, New York

Manufactured in the United States of America

Library of Congress Cataloging-in-Publication Data

Jovanovski, Meto, 1928—
    Cousins.

    Translation of: Budaletinki.
    I. Title.
PG1195.J6B813   1986   891.8′193   86–8360
ISBN 0–916515–12–5

Preface

The setting for this novel is 1917, along a World War I battlefront coinciding roughly with the present Greek-Yugoslav border. Allied French and Serbian forces to the south faced Bulgarians, who had entered the war on the side of the Central Powers. The front had been stable for over two years, with much digging and little fighting. In the summer of 1917, Greece was about to enter the war on the side of the Allies.

Breznitsa is a fictional village closely resembling Jovanovski's home of Brajchino, just south of the 1917 front. During World War I, many men of that area avoided military service by following the Macedonian tradition of leaving their villages to seek employment— usually going north to Romania. They returned home only after they had earned enough money to help their families survive the hardships of the war.

Chakarvelika had gone with her knitting out to the yard of the inn to warm her bones in the hot summer sun. Around her the hens were scratching in the debris left by the soldiers after the battle on Mount Pelister. Customers now came to the inn only for news of the casualties. The gate stood ajar, as it had been left when the army moved out of town. The dried up latrine no longer smelled. Chakarvelika sat sunning herself, dreading the winter when she would be confined to the inn and to her lonely awareness of its crackling doors and floorboards. Her husband, the lout, had left her a year after they had bought the inn. Her daughter was married and lived in a village somewhere and her son had been serving in somebody's army for the past four years.

As she knitted, she was conscious of how deeply the sun had penetrated her bones and she wondered why she hadn't started sweating. Then, quite suddenly, the two of them, Shishman and Srbin, stood before her like ghosts waiting to be seen. One was plump, dark, and sullen, the other thin, blond, and constantly chewing the smile on his lips. Chakarvelika raised her hand to her forehead and stared at them. Had her eyes been better, she might have recognized them. But she saw only their homespun trousers cut in the customary village style, and their jackets, which looked as if they

1

had been found somewhere. She recognized the knap-
sacks hanging over their shoulders. Finally, realizing
that the silent faces before her weren't going to open
their mouths, she addressed them. "What brings you
boys here?"

"We . . . ," began Shishman, the darker and shorter
one. But then he stopped as if struck by something. He
remained silent and only looked at Srbin as if he were
afraid of having done something wrong.

Then Srbin, the blond one, answered Chakarvelika.
"We're on our way home, Auntie. We've been off making money in Wallachia, up in Romania. We want to
spend the night here, if we may, and tomorrow we'll
take the road over the mountain to our village."

"When we headed north three years ago, we spent
the night here, too," Shishman added, smiling.

"I see," said Chakarvelika, and dropped her knitting
in her lap. "Where were you from, did you say?"

"From Breznitsa, Auntie," Srbin said. "I'm the son
of Sotir Vitanov—you may know him. And this man
here . . ."

"I'm Srbin's cousin, Shishman. Koté Shajkov's Shishman."

"Very good. Bless you," said Chakarvelika as she
began to squeeze the knitting in her lap. "The time has
arrived for you to come back and you're doing so, eh."

"Not really, Auntie," said Srbin. "In Romania, we
were called to the Bulgarian Consulate to be recruited.
We're coming back almost a year earlier than we
expected to."

"We didn't leave home to join the army," added
Shishman.

"Of course not," Chakarvelika said. "Didn't you have
any trouble on your way to Romania?"

"On our way up, Auntie," Srbin said, "we were
caught by the Serbs . . ."

"And given uniforms by them," said Shishman.

"But we escaped," concluded Srbin. "We weren't far from Wallachia."

"You've been lucky so far," said Chakarvelika.

"Why 'so far'?" asked Shishman, almost angrily.

"Because I don't know how you'll make it to Breznitsa," said Chakarvelika.

Shishman giggled nervously. The high, thin sound was unexpected from his massive throat.

"Over the mountain," said Srbin. "We'll cross at Griva. People from Breznitsa always cross at Griva. It's more convenient somehow. Everytime I go over, I ask myself why your people from Livadje cross at Neprtka. All of us have our own way, I suppose."

"I suppose so," mumbled Chakarvelika, shifting her knitting in her lap. Without lifting her head toward them, she said into her chin, "Your plan sounds fine, but you still can't go home. The route is a battlefield. A war is going on. The armies have closed all the roads leading there. One cannon sits next to another all along the mountain ridge. The Serbs and the French are on the far side and the Germans and Bulgarians are on this side. A bird couldn't fly over."

As soon as they understood what Chakarvelika had said, Srbin and Shishman turned their heads slowly toward the mountain, trying to see something of what they had just heard. They saw only uncertainty and turned again to Chakarvelika, as if she were their only hope. Srbin spoke. "Now, then. What's your advice, Mother?"

"How can I advise you? What can I tell you?" asked Chakarvelika. "You'll have to stay here. Sleep here. As far as food goes, I don't know. But even that won't be a problem. In no time, you'll be caught. But we'll all survive somehow."

"Who'll catch us?" demanded Shishman.

Chakarvelika remained silent for several minutes and then said to Srbin, "You must be close relatives."

"Our mothers are sisters," said Srbin.

"I knew it," said Chakarvelika. "That's why you stick together."

The cousins waited a few minutes. Shishman kept looking at Srbin as if waiting to see whether he'd gone wrong somewhere. And all that time Srbin was either swallowing dryly or smiling slightly. When his throat was completely parched, he repeated Shishman's question. "What did you mean by being caught, Mother? Who'll catch us?"

"The Bulgarians, son; they'll catch you. These days, everything that walks on two feet is a soldier. Until now you've been lucky. Let's not think about what's to come. Your bed will be there on the balcony. The hens will move to one side. Sleep to your heart's content, but when you wake up, grab a broom. The yard is a mess. If you can't think of anything to do, I'll think of something. That's settled, then," said Chakarvelika as she got up from the little chair and moved toward the door.

"What are we going to do about being caught, Mother?" Srbin persisted.

Chakarvelika neither stopped nor turned around. She went on shuffing her feet through the dirt and said in a voice that was hardly audible, "That I'll tell you, boys, when the time comes. Trust me to find the most suitable person to catch you."

The cousins sat down on the balcony without uttering a word and were still deep in thought when darkness fell. From time to time they heard people talking or somebody's wooden clogs clattering. Once in a while they heard a cart passing by. Not a soul entered the yard. Until dusk the hens pecked in the yard and on the balcony. Then the cousins settled themselves on the wooden beams and sighed occasionally, as if with relief. When the village clock struck in the dark, they didn't understand what time it was. Finally deciding it was time to sleep, they stretched out on the straw and put their hands under their heads. Then they fell asleep.

In the morning, they were awakened by the rays of the sun. Frightened by the light, they jumped to their feet. But they didn't begin work at once. Instead, they looked around and thought about their situation. Then they began sweeping the balcony where they had slept.

After a few days, they had cleared and tidied up the yard as they would have done on the eve of a market day. Chakarvelika seemed revived, livelier. She kept pacing up and down in the yard outside the inn and even worked a little herself. She fed the cousins as she would have fed laborers—breakfast, lunch, dinner, supper. She treated them to whatever she already had or could find. When they had finished with the yard, they went inside, started cleaning the loft, and ended with the kitchen, where they had dinner with Chakarvelika. Before the meal, she brought out a bottle of *rakija*.

In the afternoons, the cousins sat silently on a piece of wood under the balcony, while Chakarvelika sat with her knitting on a little stool in the middle of the yard, trying to warm her bones. Srbin and Shishman knew that the time had come to hear a new tune, and they waited almost uneasily. Chakarvelika also knew what she had to tell them, but she didn't know how. One day, just after their afternoon snack, she suddenly cried out, "Srbin!"

"Yes, Mother," Srbin replied.

Still knitting, Chakarvelika said, "Srbin, it's no good your being called 'Srbin.' You can't be called 'the Serb.' Not if you're going to be in the Bulgarian army."

"What shall I be called, then, Mother?" he asked.

"You'll be called 'Bugarin.' Can you remember that?"

"Very well, Mother," said Srbin.

Chakarvelika finished a row of knitting and didn't begin a new one. Yes, she thought, to be called "Bugarin" would be better for him. "Bugarin" was a common Macedonian name. And in Macedonian it sounded something like the word for "Bulgarian." In the Bulgarian language the two words sounded exactly the same. She removed the wool from around her neck, wound it around the woolen ball in her lap, stabbed the ball with her knitting needle, and got up. She went inside the house, but soon reappeared, her hands resting on her hips. She waddled in the direction of the cousins, but then she turned toward the gate and stopped. "Remember," she said to Srbin. "You'll be called 'Bugarin.' "

"I remember, Mother," said Srbin.

"Mother," suddenly Shishman cried out. "Should he remember it right now?"

"Right now," said Chakarvelika, "for I'm going to the Bulgarians right now to report you. If you're going to be drafted, you should always volunteer. I'll tell them it was the Serbs who tried to change your name."

The cousins exchanged glances. Chakarvelika stood still, waiting for them to say whatever they had to say to one another. Srbin spoke out, "All right, Mother. If it's better to volunteer, then let's do it."

"God help you," Chakarvelika said. She crossed herself, raised her head toward heaven, and went out the gate.

The cousins waited. They didn't even move from where they had been standing. After a while Srbin bent down, picked up a straw, split it, and began to break off bits from both ends. That seemed to remind Shishman of something he should do. He stretched his right leg forward and from his trouser pocket he produced a worn tin box that had once held shoe polish. Srbin knew what was going on and yet watched his cousin without a word. He saw Shishman carefully wipe the outside of the little tin box against his trousers. Then he opened it, blew hard into both sides of the box, and closed it again. After that he spoke. "Brother, I'm beginning to panic again. If you don't mind, I'll put a pebble in the box."

"I don't mind," said Srbin.

They both began to look in front of them for a suitable pebble, but couldn't find one. Shishman got up and followed his eyes to a spot a short distance away. Srbin went after him. With stooped backs they paced the yard, looking left and right, and moving away from each other. With backs still bent, they reached the farthest end of the yard, then turned around and moved forward, until they were face to face. Occasionally they found something to consider, or, if unsatisfactory, to throw away. When their heads met, they stopped, knelt down, and looked at each other. They opened their pebble-filled palms and tried to settle on the best specimen. Shishman, indecisive as usual, took the one chosen by his cousin. He placed it carefully in the middle of the tin box and then closed it. When the pebble inside rattled insistently, Shishman looked at his cousin with joy and giggled quietly.

Then Chakarvelika, followed by a mustachioed Bulgarian sergeant, appeared at the gate. The surprised cousins, their mouths frozen open, rose slowly to their feet. Shishman carefully slipped the tin box containing the pebble into his pocket. Filled with dread, they stiffened, then shivered. The pebble in Shishman's pocket rattled, but made no impression on the others. In the meantime, Chakarvelika led the sergeant toward them. They stood face to face, he before them and they with their backs almost touching the wall surrounding the yard of the inn.

The sergeant put his hands behind his back and stood with his legs apart; they were wound with white cloth and tied with leather laces. He filled his lungs with air as he prepared to ask his first question in a proper manner. But when Shishman straightened up, intending to imitate the sergeant's position of military attention, the pebble in his pocket rattled and the sergeant's lungs collapsed. Startled, the sergeant tried to remain cool. He pulled himself together quickly and said, in Bulgarian, "So, it's you two who've been sent to our regiment."

"It's us," said Srbin.

"It's us," Shishman echoed.

"Aha," said the sergeant. "Which one of you is B'lgarin?"

"We are both Bulgarian, sir," said Shishman, as he jumped into the air. The pebble in the box in his pocket rattled.

Although the noise didn't anger the sergeant, it startled him. He drew in his breath and spoke clearly, "I'm asking which one of you is called 'Bugarin'?"

"I am, sir," said Srbin.

"Aha," said the sergeant. He twisted the end of his mustache, and shifted his weight from one leg to the other. It was obvious he wanted to say something important. Shishman, also agitated, shifted his weight from one foot to the other. As he did so, the pebble in his pocket rattled again. The sergeant looked at him, reassured himself, and spoke in a calmer voice than he himself expected. He addressed Srbin. "Madame, here, explained to me everything about your name and how the Serbs changed it to Srbin when they captured you. The dirty Serbs are capable of doing anything. As is evident in your case, they have changed your name to try to claim that you're a Serb."

"Quite right, sir," said Srbin.

"But nothing can help those bastards. The proof is in your readiness to . . ."

The pebble in Shishman's pocket started to rattle as his legs began to shake.

"What's the matter with you?" the Bulgarian asked angrily.

"Nothing, sir. It's only a little tin box."

"A little tin box with a pebble in it," explained Srbin.

Shishman took the box out of his pocket. The rattling stopped when he clasped the box between his thumb and index finger. He held it out toward the sergeant. The sergeant was obviously curious, and yet he dared not take it.

"Take it, sir," said Shishman. "Look at it, if you wish."

"Look at it! Look at it!" said Srbin.

"Hmmmm," said the Bulgarian.

"Here," said Shishman and, to be helpful, he opened the box, held it out toward the sergeant and shook the pebble. It didn't make an attractive sound now that the box was open. Suddenly the sergeant looked as if he understood. He spoke in a sharp voice. "Put that toy away! Can't you see we're discussing most important matters? So," he resumed, "Madame explained everything to me. Therefore, come with me. We'll have time to say a few more things to each other. Madame," he turned to Chakarvelika, "Madame, Mother Bulgaria is most grateful to you."

"Don't mention it," said Chakarvelika with restraint.

Now it was time to set off. Srbin and Shishman looked stonily at each other. They said goodbye to Chakarvelika and followed the sergeant. Shishman shoved his hand in his pocket. He grabbed tight hold of

the tin box to muffle the rattle and to suppress the
agitation that had seized him.

As they passed through the gate of the yard, Chakarvelika crossed herself three times and prayed for their
good health and safe journey.

Chakarvelika had done her job well, for Srbin and
Shishman found themselves quickly outfitted in Bulgarian uniforms. Lion-shaped insignia decorated their
khaki hats and their legs were bound with strips of
cloth tied on with leather cords. But still they were not
given rifles. They were told they would get them at the
front lines. The cousins accepted all explanations. From
time to time, as they waited for further orders, they
looked at each other with half-opened mouths. It was
clear to them that they were to go straight to the front.
They wanted to know what was in the big sealed envelope which they had been told to guard as they would
guard their own eyes and to give over, untouched, to
the leader of their assigned unit. The last question they
were asked was whether they preferred to eat in camp
or to be given a packed lunch and set off right away.
After brief consultation, the cousins agreed they'd take
a packed lunch.

"We aren't used to cooked meals, anyway," said
Srbin.

"Indeed we aren't," confirmed Shishman.

At noon, they headed up the mountain on the main
road. They stopped at the first fountain and opened
their lunch. Many people, most of them soldiers, were
passing up and down the road; occasionally a donkey
or a mule could be seen. Then, a cart pulled by oxen
passed them. A few peasants, probably from nearby
villages, walked by as well. But none stopped at the
fountain. Some would greet the cousins with a lift of a
hand or a nod of the head, and continue on their way.

When the cousins finished eating, they packed up the rest of their food, but they did not stand up immediately to resume their journey. Instead, they sat in silence until an elderly peasant came for a drink of water. He came to the fountain and hesitated before the two soldiers. When he had convinced himself that they wouldn't object to his presence, he stepped forward and cupped his hand to have a drink of water. As he wiped his mouth, Srbin addressed him. "Are you from a neighboring village, Uncle?"

Startled, the old man looked at them both and asked, "What! You're *our* folk, are you?"

"We are. From across the mountain."

"I see," said the old man. "They've brought you real close."

"Close, indeed," said Srbin, "but . . ."

Lost in thought, the old man began to wipe his mouth again. "But why?"

Srbin pointed toward the mountain at his back. "All this is a front line."

The old man looked at one and then the other. Then he looked around himself. Again he looked at the cousins. "Lads," he said, "a bird can't fly over the mountain. A man would have to be lucky . . . Only if he can find a hole in the darkness," he added.

"True," said Srbin.

"Yes," confirmed the old man. "And," he said, "I wanted to ask you which village over the mountain you came from. But, since you didn't ask me, it might be better if we each went our own way as if we'd never met."

"It's better," said Shishman.

The old man had walked some distance before the cousins dared to glance at one another. They shrugged their shoulders and got up to go.

They walked slowly, step by step. If they were caught

by the night, they would take the blankets off their
shoulders and sleep in a field along the road. If they
reached their destination . . . Well, they reassured
themselves, they would.

For now, in silence, each one for himself, they thought
about the envelope that Srbin carried in his shirt. All
Shishman's hope focused on his cousin. He restrained
himself from saying anything, but looked at Srbin again
and again. Finally, Srbin spoke. "Forget it! We can do
nothing."

"Why not?" asked Shishman.

"Well," said Srbin, "what's the use of struggling to
open the envelope to no purpose?"

They went on. Neither thought of stopping to have a
rest. If they were seen sitting, somebody might start
asking questions about this and that, and they might
say something wrong. Therefore they walked as slowly
as possible and did not complain of being tired. Nothing escaped their eyes. They searched the area above
the road all the way up to the mountain ridge, but could
see nothing. They knew that the battlefront was somewhere up there—two armies opposing one another.
The idea made them uneasy. They imagined that a
cannon, either by chance or by someone's intention,
could roar at any moment and frighten them.

As the sun began to set, the silence became even
more tense. They walked closer and closer to each
other. If they noticed anyone coming their way, they
moved to the opposite side of the road and greeted the
stranger from a distance. They avoided becoming
involved in conversation. Alone again, they fixed their
eyes on the mountain ridge. They gazed so intensely
that Shishman couldn't help saying, "Breznitsa is right
over the mountain, isn't it?"

Srbin looked fearfully at his cousin to see if, by any
chance, he was pointing with his finger. Then, calmly,

he replied, "It only looks so to you. The mountain is steep and the woods are thick."

"It must be," said Shishman, "but to me, when I looked, it seemed quite near."

"It's far," said Srbin abruptly.

"So it is," agreed Shishman, and felt a slight sorrow in his heart for starting a conversation that had annoyed Srbin.

They had thought so little about the village they had been ordered to go to that they were surprised when they reached it. The village wasn't yet in sight, but the cousins recognized its familiar smell when the breeze was right, and thought they heard the voices of people and the movement of cattle. The cousins became so excited, it seemed to them that their feet hardly touched the ground. Shishman sniffled quietly.

"Cousin, will I need a pebble for the tin box?"

"I don't think so," said Srbin.

They pressed on. Suddenly, the road turned to the left and sloped down toward the river. When they came around the bend in the river, they saw the first houses of the village, nestled under the verdant slope of the mountain. At the same time, they became aware of the roaring of the river. Somewhere below them, on a country road, a calf in search of its mother bellowed. The setting sun, reflected against the sharp edge of the horizon on the mountain, blinded them. A few more steps and they were in shade. The veil of smoke above the houses became visible amid the thick green leaves. The thought of what might be going on under the roofs and behind the bushes and trees stirred their yearning and flooded them with pain and sorrow.

"Me," said Shishman almost decisively, "if I find a suitable pebble, I'll take it."

Srbin stopped without saying a word and looked at the ground around him. "Here," he said quickly. As they set off toward the village, he said, "If you can wait, don't put it in the box immediately."

"All right," agreed Shishman.

After they had passed some high bushes, the road branched off to the right. The river roared more and more loudly. Soon they came to a wooden bridge and a road, its direction invisible because of the growing darkness. Under the bridge, on the other side of the river, about ten soldiers were doing their washing. Further on along the road, they met groups of soldiers sitting down to rest. An elderly villager or two sat among them.

The cousins were directed to a large house, plastered and painted white, its roof outlined with blue gutters. There were two balconies, one above the other. It was undoubtedly the house of someone who had made his fortune abroad. In front of the gate a guard stopped them. He began to ask them questions, but soon lost interest. Then he pulled a rope and rang a bell that sounded like a frightened goat in flight.

In the yard, they were met by a soldier who blocked their way. He held a small knife in one hand and an apple in the other. Slowly, he cut slices of apple and placed them in his mouth. In between bites he spoke. "Speak up; speak up," he said as he waved the hand that held the knife. He had no time for questions. Obviously, he wasn't interested in the cousins. When he had finished eating the apple, he carefully wiped the little knife with his two fingers, folded it, and put it in his pocket. Then he wiped his mouth with his hand and rubbed his palms dry on his trousers. All the time he continued chewing.

"We were told to report to the commanding officer," said Srbin.

"Wait here," he said to the cousins as he took the sealed envelope and disappeared into the house.

The cousins waited patiently. Since the guard at the gate had his eyes fixed on them, they avoided looking around. They had no interest in seeing anything they shouldn't. Srbin, tall and thin, stood still as a saint, while Shishman shifted his impressive weight from one foot to the other. He constantly turned his ear toward Srbin, as if he expected his cousin to whisper something in confidence. Srbin, without even a blink, gazed at the door, waiting for the soldier to come back. Suddenly, the soldier called to them from the lower balcony. He motioned for them to come up.

The cousins, Srbin in front, Shishman after him, entered the house and climbed up the corner wooden staircase to the floor where the soldier was waiting for them. He pointed to the door they were to enter and moved to make way for them. The cousins gave him a look of surprise. Then in order to help, he reached over to knock at the door, and then moved aside again. The cousins looked blankly at each other. When they heard somebody shout from inside, they shuddered very slightly. The soldier opened the door for them and moved out of the way once again.

Opposite the door, in the middle of the room, sat a hatless officer at a dining table. His face, with its thin mustache, was the face of a barber. Shishman, full of fear and respect, immediately fixed his eyes on the officer's hat, which, like a dog sitting obediently on its hind legs, rested on its visor on the table in front of the officer. Srbin remembered to salute, and simultaneously bashed Shishman's ribs with his elbow. The blow made him jump like a loose spring. He opened his mouth to say something, but all his words vanished.

The "barber" watched them for a while. Then he asked in Bulgarian, "Which one of you two is the wretch?"

"We both are," said Shishman. He was too hasty.

"I know that," said the barber. "I'm asking who's Srbin, the Serb?"

"I'm not a Serb. I'm a Bulgarian, sir," said Srbin.

"I know," said the barber, "but look what those bastards we're fighting against have done to you. They've disgraced you for the rest of your life."

He got up. He said he would take them to the other gentlemen, the other officers. He put on his hat and tightened his belt. They went out into the corridor, where the guard was slicing another apple. He stood at attention while the officer passed, and then winked at the cousins.

In the next room they found themselves before four other officers who were sitting on the four sides of a wooden bed, each turned to face the back of another. They were playing cards. They stopped the game, but didn't get up, and just stared at the cousins. Srbin and Shishman stiffened in attention, as the sergeant in the town had taught them, but the result was only a feeble stiffening and shrinking of their necks.

"Is this supposed to be a salute?" asked one of the four.

"Beg your pardon, sir," said Srbin, bowing his head. "We're new. That's why."

"I know how. Now I remember," said Shishman unexpectedly.

"Let's see it then."

Shishman had remembered how to salute, and at that moment he wanted to show off. Then he saw one of the officers taking advantage of the situation by stealing a card from the heap in the middle. Shishman stared in disbelief and completely forgot what he was trying to do.

"They'll learn," said the one who had stolen the card. He stood up, went to the window, and picked up some papers. The cousins recognized an envelope left on the table, and knew that these were the papers they had brought. They looked at each other as if admitting their mistake. The officer read the papers. "Pero Shajkov?"

"That's me," said Shishman.

"Aha," said the officer. "So you aren't the one."

"Yes I am, sir," interrupted Shishman. "Everybody calls me Shishman. That's why you think I'm not the one."

The officers look puzzled. The one who had stolen the card looked at the papers again and asked, "Which one of you two is B'lgarin?"

"We both are," said Srbin.

"Cross my heart," said Shishman.

"I'm asking who's called 'Bugarin'?"

"Me," said Srbin.

"He is," said Shishman, helpfully. He seemed to want to point at his cousin, but in doing so, he accidently dropped the pebble he had held in case of need. Because the pebble was round, it rolled easily on the wooden floor and came close to one of the officer's boots; then it bounced against the other boot and returned in front of Shishman to the exact spot where it had first fallen. The officers watched the path of the pebble in amazement and then looked at Shishman in disbelief.

"What's that?" asked the barber.

Shishman shrugged his shoulders. "A pebble," he said.

The officers felt uneasy, for it really was a pebble. Nevertheless, the scheduled procedure of the meeting had been disrupted.

The situation was saved by a fat officer who had remained seated on the bed. Suddenly he fell backward. Getting up couldn't have been easy for him. When he decided to try, he first bent forward with difficulty and then, like a bear, supported himself on his hands. He shuffled on his buttocks until his short legs touched the floor, and then, with a tremendous effort, tried to stand erect. Still holding the cards in one hand, he butted one of the officers with his head as he rose, and when he had pushed him away, he stood before the cousins. With one hand on his back, and swaying precariously, he addressed Srbin. "Do you have a picture of yourself?"

"A picture? My God, sir! What would I need a picture for?"

"You don't even have a picture of yourself?"

"Not even of myself, sir."

"Forget it," said the fat man. "We'll have you photographed." He spoke and then stepped backward and looked intently at the other officers. "Gentlemen, I have an idea. I'll write an article with the title, 'I am Bulgarian and Bugarin is my name.' Then we'll attach this man's photograph and send it to the newspaper *Fatherland*."

The barber's eyes shone. "Fantastic!" he said. "One word, two meanings."

"On the contrary," said the fat man. "Two words, one meaning."

The cousins, of course, understood nothing. Their only worry was their inability to sense whether anything bad was about to happen to them. They were frightened that they might not know what was coming. They could hardly wait to be left alone so they could think. But in the army there is little time for thinking. The soldier who had been eating apples took them to the yard and there, in the dark, they waited for another soldier to lead them to the place where they would spend the night. They couldn't see the soldier in the dark, but they could hear him making noises, eating, chopping something, or scratching himself. They had the sense that although they couldn't see him, he could tell every time they blinked. When the other soldier came, he led them hurriedly through the village while the cousins stumbled and jumped over stones on the unfamiliar path. Then the soldier led them out of the village, into a field. There he reported to somebody who didn't even try to see them in the dark.

"Very well," he said. "Let them lie down anywhere and we'll deal with them tomorrow."

When the cousins began to look for a place to sit down, they realized they were in a veritable anthill of soldiers. They sensed that hundreds of soldiers surrounded them, and they dared not go too far, for they might lose each other. They didn't see anyone whose face they might be able to recognize in daylight. As they continued to circle in one place, one of the soldiers approached them and asked if they intended to stand up all night. Then they knelt down obediently and sat on the very spot in which they had been standing. Stiff and perplexed, they remained sitting for a long time. Although the sky above them was clear, everything around them was filled with mystery. Darkness blurred the shapes of one uncertainty into another. The noises and sounds coming from the sleeping soldiers reached their ears and echoed like a moaning of the earth.

"Let's lie down, shall we?" Srbin whispered, taking the blanket off his shoulders."

"I can't," said Shishman. "I'm sitting on a stone."

Srbin moved away and made room for him. After some struggle, they settled down and fell asleep.

The next morning, the cousins realized there weren't as many soldiers as they had believed the night before. Still, the day wasn't pleasant. Different commands were cried out on all sides, and dogs seemed to be barking all the time. The cousins felt cold, and as soon as the sun had warmed them, they felt drowsy. They wanted to find out many things, but dared ask nothing. Everything seemed somewhat unpleasant, yet not what one would expect of a battlefield. Later, as they sat on a wall high above the road and slopped their watery broth at lunch, Shishman said, "Surely the shooting of the rifles and machine guns can't be heard here, can it?"

"Who knows?" said Srbin.

That was the most puzzling thing to them. The front line, as Chakarvelika had said, was somewhere here, along the ridge of the mountain, but they heard no shots. No wounded or dead men were being brought in. They couldn't imagine a battlefield without the roar of cannons, either.

"Why do you think the cannons aren't being fired?" Shishman asked later.

"I don't know," said Srbin.

After a pause, Shishman found an explanation. "They're probably fired every second day. Maybe even once a week."

"Maybe," said Srbin.

While they were still wondering about everything they could think of or see, they noticed that the field was slowly becoming empty. In company after company, the soldiers were going somewhere. By snack time, the leader of the company they now seemed to be part of called for his men. He lined them up, inspected them, and sent a soldier with his report. Shishman was uneasy. He stiffened. Frightened to look behind him, he began to roll his eyes from side to side. The men were lined up in two rows, he in front, Srbin behind him. He couldn't ask his cousin the question he had in mind. Meanwhile, the soldier who had taken the report somewhere came back with a companion. At that very moment Shishman saw a perfect pebble in front of him. But could he bend down? The soldier rejoined the line, and the one who had come with him stood next to the leader of the company. The company leader shouted a command: "Attention!"

While everyone else sprang to attention, Shishman bent down quickly, grabbed the pebble, and stood up. The officer saw him, but said nothing. He only seemed to take a deeper breath. They faced right and set off. Then they took a steep path, came to the main road, and walked steadily uphill. While they marched, Shishman put the pebble away in the tin box. As they walked up the road, the pebble rattled against the sides of the box in Shishman's pocket. He was pleased with himself, but he didn't know Srbin's thoughts since he hadn't been able to ask his opinion. Now, when he had already acted, he turned around and looked at his cousin. Srbin smiled at him and Shishman, as usual, was happy.

The company walked through a village and, at the bridge above it, they took the path up the mountain. Shishman and Srbin turned and looked at each other. They shrugged their shoulders and, accepting their fate, went on. The path led them higher and higher. Always they bore to the right until they reached the top of the ridge and saw the lake in the valley on the other side of the mountain beneath them. They imagined they could see their village.

"They're taking us there," said Shishman, meaning the front line.

"More than likely," said Srbin, grimacing. Shishman winced.

The sun went down; then night fell, and it became dark. Colors in the lake changed continuously, and finally assumed a strange glitter that suggested coldness. The company went on. They didn't stop, as many of them had hoped they would. Later, without a command, the officer abruptly faced the marching unit. The

soldiers, caught by surprise, crashed into each others'
backs.

"Gather closely around me," said the officer. "You
have a short break while I explain something. We're
approaching the battlefront where we're going to relieve
those fighting. They'll withdraw for a deserved rest.
The minute we resume our journey, remember this: I
don't want to hear even a squeak! That's all! Proceed,"
said the officer, and he marched off.

The company followed him. In less than a minute the
noise caused by the stopping and setting off again had
grown faint. Only dull strides and the rattle of Shishman's pebble could be heard—almost certainly by the
officer. Shishman wondered what to do. He wanted to
ask Srbin's advice. Suddenly the officer stepped aside.
With appropriate commands, he marched the company
past him single file. The rattling of the pebble was
getting nearer and nearer his ear. As Shishman passed,
the officer grabbed him by his shoulder and pulled him
out of line with a strength one wouldn't have expected
from his haggard appearance. *Tack-tack-tackrrr-tack,*
rattled the pebble in the tin box.

"You idiot!" said the company leader. "Does that
rattle come from your head or from somewhere else?"

"It's only a pebble, sir," said Shishman, putting his
hand in his pocket.

"Give it here," said the officer.

Shishman took the box out of his pocket with a
shaking hand and gave it to him. In the dark, the officer
couldn't see what he held. It rattled in his hand. Angry,
he flung it down the hill, over the heads of his men. The
tin box rattled loudly, then went quiet for a while, and
groaned once more when it touched the ground somewhere below.

"Proceed now," said the commanding officer as he
hurried to the front of the line.

Shishman felt sorry for the tin box, but when the commanding officer told him to join the column, he was terrified. Srbin had surely gone ahead somewhere and he would have to creep in between two strangers. God knows what he would have done if Srbin, who had stood aside to wait for him, hadn't grabbed him by his arm.

Soon they arrived at an unknown destination. To Srbin and Shishman, it was nowhere. They were in the heart of a forest, and they hadn't met a soul. The order was to keep silent and wait. Only the officer who had led them went a bit further. They had been waiting for quite a while when he came back with two other soldiers. The two who came took two others from the company. The rest of them waited for two others to come and lead two more away. The cousins, just in case, stayed to the side until they realized that in this incomprehensible coming and going they could be separated. They simply stuck to each other in the dark and kept their distance from the others as much as they could until, finally, they were taken together. As soon as they set off, Shishman's heart sank. "Cousin, I have neither a pebble nor a box."

"Keep quiet now," Srbin said to him.

They walked through the forest for a while and then found themselves in a more open area. Hidden by bushes, the soldiers gave them rifles to hold. The soldiers, who sounded angry, took the cousins into a deep trench and marched along it for a while. Then they were almost running. But since the trench turned several times, the cousins couldn't tell in what direction they were being led.

The soldiers positioned Srbin first. While one of them remained with him, the other one took Shishman a few meters further along in a sort of cove so small he couldn't even turn around. Then the soldier explained

what he was to do: "Get the rifle ready to fire. Keep
your eyes peeled. Look in front of you and be ready for
the enemy to appear. If shots come from the opposite
side, you shoot as well. If you see anything approaching, give a signal. That's all. The main thing, you understand, is that it's either him or you! Good luck!"

Shishman neither heard nor understood anything of
the soldier's instructions. He simply felt pain in his
forehead, as if he had already been hit with a bullet.
He rubbed his head nervously with his hand, but the
pain spread across his head to his temples and he felt
his stomach getting heavy. He looked helplessly toward
Srbin, whose shadow he could imagine rather than
actually see. The chirping of the crickets was getting
louder. A few times, he tried to gaze before him in the
direction of the enemy, but the very thought made him
blind. Occasionally he would muster enough courage
to look, but he could see nothing, for his head began to
spin and his eyes became dim. He felt as if his big,
clumsy body, from which his soul wanted to escape,
was like a stone around his neck. He wanted to cry like
a child, but was afraid of causing trouble for his cousin
Srbin. He felt better when he could feel some pebbles
on the ground under his palm. He preoccupied himself
with looking for a suitable pebble to put in the box he
didn't have. Nothing else interested him anymore. He
felt drowsy, and he was torn between the thought of
the pebble and the box and his resistance to his sleep-
iness. The chirping of the crickets was getting louder
and louder. It was lulling him to sleep. Then it would
disappear for a while and then wake him up again.
Every time he became mesmerized by the chirping,
space seemed endless. The air was intoxicating, and
the lake beneath him beamed with hope. Except for
the trench and the uniform, he felt as he had when he

was out with the sheep at Breznitsa. His rifle pointed in that direction now.

Srbin watched peacefully as the darkness eroded the details of the shapes in the landscape before him and, like dew, sank drop by drop into the ground. In front of the trenches, on a steep slope of barren hill, there were a few scattered bushes and many narrow paths criss-crossed like a cobweb. At the foot of the hill, beside the lake, there was a field that made its way up another long hill. Behind that field lay the cousins' village, Breznitsa. Before his eyes Srbin saw everything just as he knew it, from this hill where he had never been before. Only the enemy could not be seen. It was hard to believe that the front was actually here. He wanted to believe that all this military business was some kind of hocus-pocus.

He tried to judge the position of the front line, and came to the conclusion that his uncle's village must be near it. As children, he and Shishman often used to go visiting there. Once, he recalled, some children had talked them into climbing this barren hillside all the way up to a little church—which must be somewhere lower down—that could be seen from the village. He wanted to exchange a glance with his cousin, but when he look toward him, he saw that Shishman was still fast asleep, with his arms out of the trench. He wanted to wake him up, but when he realized that there wasn't anyone around to be angry, he stopped worrying. Srbin had thought of throwing a little stone, but that might frighten his cousin and make him shout when he woke up. He had no idea what to do and hoped that maybe Shishman would soon wake up by himself. At sunrise the mountain ridge shone in the new light. The light distracted Srbin, so that he wasn't aware that the corporal had appeared behind Shishman.

Shishman smiled at the corporal as he opened his eyes.

"Sleeping, eh?" asked the corporal.

"No," said Shishman.

"Then why do you hold your rifle as if you were ready to throw it away?" he asked. The corporal stretched over Shishman's head and grabbed the rifle. He withdrew into the adjacent trench and looked at it. "It's jammed," the corporal said reproachfully.

He unjammed it, then opened it. He carefully pulled the catch back so he wouldn't drop the shell on the ground, but nothing came out and the corporal realized that Shishman's rifle was not loaded. "It's empty!" he said, flabbergasted, and rolled his eyes in disgust.

Shishman tried to explain. "I was afraid it would go off accidentally during the night, sir. I didn't want to make any trouble. I'll load it right away," he said earnestly and stretched his hand toward the rifle.

The corporal clenched his teeth, but realizing that nothing Shishman could do at that moment would satisfy him, he decided not to forget him. He handed Shishman his rifle and ordered him to resume his post. Then he walked down the trench. Shishman, with his arms spread out in front of him, lifted himself up on his toes to look at Srbin, but right at that moment he saw the corporal was standing beside his cousin. The soldier said something to Srbin and then left. Stooping down, Srbin left his post and set off toward Shishman. He already knew everything.

"You fell asleep," he said to his cousin. "Come on now."

"Where to?" asked Shishman.

During the day it was customary for the soldiers to leave their posts and spend their time in a huge hole that had been dug out of the side of the hill and looked like a lime pit. Since the front here had been quiet for a long time, the soldiers had had time to dig out the hillside with trenches, both along the front and in the direction of the retreat and access lines. During the day, there were only sentries and scouts along the front who communicated by a network of ropes that could be pulled to the left and right by the chain of soldiers. The end rope rang the bell in a cave that was supplied with telephone connections and set up as headquarters. All this was explained to them by the leader of the company the first morning they left their posts at the front. However, he said he wanted to perfect the system by appointing one soldier to move continually from sentry to sentry. This measure would serve as a precaution against failure of the rope system.

The solders liked the new system. It not only enabled them to walk in a wider circle, but it meant having a pair of binoculars so they could satisfy their curiosity about the life of the enemy. Thus they could confirm any gossip circulating among the soldiers and add more flavor to it. In fact, the French were well concealed, so very little could be seen. But according to rumor, their life, in contrast to life on this side of the front line, sounded like an operetta. The French lay idle much of the time, had showers installed, were allotted an unlimited number of cigarettes, and drank cocoa like water. The Bulgarian soldiers were encouraged to fantasize about the life of the French in this manner. They saw the French as pampered weaklings who could easily be beaten by their hardened Bulgarian comrades.

"Do you really think," the company commander would say, "that we live the way we do because we're poor and have chosen this way of life? No, fellow soldiers! Bulgaria is much better off! But Bulgaria wants tough soldiers. Which dog is more threatening: the spoiled and overfed one or the scavenger who takes care of himself?"

Srbin and Shishman weren't interested in any of that. When they had the binoculars, they preferred to look at the hill opposite them. Breznitsa was behind it. They were eager for something familiar to come in their sight, but even through the glasses the objects lost their shapes and were transformed into indefinite blurs. The less they saw, the more they recognized in their thoughts. They mixed with no one. Whenever they could, they dropped to the bottom of the trench and remained there, silent for hours. Even if they exchanged a word or two, their thoughts were always far away.

Sitting relaxed at the bottom of the trench on the dry, rusty red soil, his legs apart and stretched out, Shishman either dug with his heel or scraped the earth in front of him with a nail, looking for a pebble, like a dog scheming to hide its bone. Srbin looked sleepy all the time. He sat with his hands between his legs, his knees bent into his stomach, his hat over his closed eyes. It was enough for the cousins to be together and alone. Thus they pondered over the same thing, the only thing, and rested from the thoughts that burdened them and felt as heavy as a mountain.

"Eh," said Shishman, determined to dig out the pebble he'd found.

"Ah?" asked Srbin with his eyes closed.

"Nothing. If I only had the pebble . . ."

"There are as many pebbles as you wish here."

"But I haven't got a tin box."

"What if you had one?"

"It would have been different."

"Different, my foot!" said Srbin, blinking.

Shishman gave him a sad look. "Don't say that," he said pleadingly.

Srbin didn't reply.

Shishman added, "I understand. You're upset."

"Of course I am."

The sarcastic soldier with the funny name came toward them. He was called Peyou. His little eyes were half closed, as if he suspected something. He always wore a forced smile on his face. Sometimes he would frown for a moment and wrinkle his nose, but then he would smile again immediately to conceal his real feelings. But he never smiled with his whole mouth. He often looked contentedly at the cousins. They became frightened at the very thought of him. This time he nearly crushed them as he moved toward them.

"Hee-hee," he gurgled. "Everything going well, eh?"

Srbin opened his eyes, straightened himself up, and lifted his hat. Shishman only lifted his eyes toward the intruder and stuck his finger in the hole he was digging.

As Peyou opened his mouth, he went on smiling in a teasing way, and shifted his eyes from one to the other. But he didn't move. To provoke them, he stayed a painfully long time. Once Shishman lowered his eyes and while Srbin was watching, he continued digging a pebble out of a hole.

"Everything's O.K.," said Shishman, "but I find these little stones most difficult. The red soil is very hard."

"That's why it's good for bricks."

"You know how to make them?" asked Srbin.

Peyou scratched behind his ear with his index finger and broadened his smile. "Maybe I do," he said as he moved away.

The cousins exchanged glances and stood looking at one another for a long time. Then once again Srbin relaxed and Shishman went on with the work before him.

The futility of the thought of Breznitsa tired the cousins. They often remembered Kolenovo and their uncle and aunt, but outside of that, they could think of

little else but Breznitsa, in spite of the mountain bar-
rier between them. They were happy when they faced
the village.

One day Srbin grabbed Shishman by his sleeve and
drew him outside of the trench. They climbed out and
into the bushes, sat behind a rock, and gazed toward
their uncle and aunt's village. The village was out of
sight, down behind the hill, beside the lake. Only a
cloud of gray smoke was hanging peacefully above it,
like the eaves of a house. Putting down their rifles, they
sat with their knees under their chins and gazed toward
the village from under their eyebrows. Shishman began
to wrinkle his nose as he sniffed the air. "I can smell...,"
he said.

"... hot bread and cowshit," said Srbin.

"Ummmmmm," said Shishman.

"You're only imagining it," said Srbin. He was also
beginning to become aware of that smell in his own
nose.

They were pleased with the change in their routine
and now, whenever they could, they would wander
from the trenches and sit above the rock. The new sight
seemed more real to them. They didn't know why, but
they were hopeful.

On Sundays, the soldiers would go in groups to a
spring deep in the woods. They even walked down the
ravine to the monastery. On some days, they were
either visited by adjacent companies, or they visited
one of the others. They were told that the company
before theirs had had a flute player and that the off-
duty soldiers would go to a field to dance. But in their
own company, nobody but Shishman could play the
flute.

"Surely a flute can be found," said Shishman.

"Surely," said Srbin.

Then they were silent. Shishman spoke again. "Well? What do you say?"

"About what?"

"The flute!"

"Nothing," said Srbin.

"I agree," said Shishman after a pause. Finally, after a number of hestitations, they decided not to mention the subject. Neither wanted to destroy the peaceful atmosphere, unless both of them could benefit by it.

The cousins became obsessed by a desire to visit their relatives at Kolenovo. They had been going to their place above the rock for the past few days, and there they could think of nothing else. They felt dizzy and sick from all their concentration on how they could get to the village. They had no trouble suggesting new and different plans, but their suggestions never seemed like reasonable possibilities. From time to time, Shishman would wave his hand and speak.

"Ah!"

"Eh?"

"Nothing. I thought I might come up with something."

"I know," Srbin said. "Thinking is like digging. When you start, the shovel feels like a feather in your hands, but later it feels like it was filled with lead."

"True enough," said Shishman. "My mother never learned to knit even a sock. She'd always make a mistake counting the stitches, and that was that!"

Still, the cousins weren't in a hurry. As soon as the thinking tired him, Srbin would sit under an oak tree, pull his hat over his face, and shut his eyes, while Shishman pulled moss off a rock, as if he were weeding.

One day they saw the leader's orderly behind the bushes below them. Although they watched him from under their eyes, they pretended not to notice him. He was fat, swaying on his legs and moving his arms for balance. He looked like a turtle flying above the bushes.

He was coming straight toward them, occasionally waving his hand at them, calling them. The cousins didn't move. Breathless, he stopped at the slope beside the rock. He leaned his thigh and one hand against the rock, and with the sleeve of the other arm he wiped his sweating forehead. Winded and perspiring, he barely managed to look at Srbin and point his hand at him. When he finally found a moment between breaths, he managed to say, "You!"

Srbin gave Shishman a sign.

"Me?" Shishman asked, startled.

The orderly waved his hand in despair. "Not you, but the Bulgarian!"

Shishman whined, "I'm Bulgarian too."

The orderly took several quick breaths and then said, "I don't care about your lies, you bastards. I only came to tell the one who calls himself Bulgarian to go and see the leader of the company right away."

After this, the orderly seemed relieved. He recovered his breath, cooled himself down a bit, and started back without a word. In order to prevent himself from rolling downhill, he jumped as he walked along.

Srbin wasn't in a hurry. He gazed out toward the mountains above the lake. Shishman, staring at him, waited like a baby crow hungry for worms. The palm of his right hand was already pressed against the ground to support himself, and he held his rifle in his left hand, ready to get up and follow Srbin.

"A lizard!" said Srbin.

"Where is it?" Shishman looked, bewildered.

Lizards weren't favorites with Shishman. He couldn't see one without feeling the impulse to throw a stone at it. It was rare for him not to hit it in the head with his first throw. The lizard's forelegs were peeping out of a corner of the rock. Shishman saw it, got up, and turned around to find a suitable stone. In the meantime, however, Srbin scared it away by throwing a tiny piece of wood.

"Why did you scare it off?" asked Shishman sadly.

"I felt sorry for it," said Srbin as he got up.

They set off, Srbin in front, Shishman after him.

Srbin thought that the picture-taking and the newspaper stories were some kind of a joke, but this was the reason that they had summoned him. Actually, Shishman had known of it before Srbin had. When Srbin went inside the cave, Shishman stayed outside with the orderly, who was sitting on a stone holding the back of his neck with one hand. He was still panting.

"They'll have his photo taken," puffed the orderly.

"How will they do it?"

"I don't know. They'll do it somehow. A man has come specially."

"I know," said Shishman.

The orderly looked at him curiously. "How do you know?"

Shishman feared that he might have gotten himself into deep water. "I know," he said. His words gave him a tone of authority. "I know many things. You look at me and you say to yourself, 'He's a fool,' don't you?" Shishman's voice was serious and worried.

The fat man looked at him with pressed lips, as if he were hesitating about something. He began to scratch his head. Then he asked, "What do you think?"

"I think you're a fool," said Shishman.

Perplexed, the orderly scratched his head again. "Maybe I am," he said bravely. "So what?"

"Nothing," said Shishman. "The main thing to know is that it doesn't matter if you're a fool. That's what I wanted to tell you. But now you are going to get mad."

"Me? Get mad?" The orderly responded immediately. "God forbid! They all make fun of me, but I don't remember ever getting mad. I just stop to think for a moment—that's all."

"It's because you're clever. That's why."

"How's that? Fool and clever at the same time?"

"You think it's impossible?" Shishman asked seriously.

"I don't know," said the orderly. "You know what I say? If stupidity and wisdom are like water and milk, it's possible. But if they are like water and oil, it cannot be possible."

The conversation was becoming too philosophical for both of them, but fortunately, Srbin soon came out of the cave. He was followed by the photographer, the leader of the company, two sergeants, and the corporal.

The photographer walked away from the group, then stopped and faced them. He signaled them to stay while he began to inspect the hole that looked like a lime pit. "I should photograph him in a fighting position," he said.

First he looked around. Then he looked at Srbin, who stood waiting. He was all bundled up as if he were packaged, ready for posting somewhere. The photographer stroked his chin, scratched his neck, and smacked his lips. Then he fixed his eyes on Srbin. "Good," said the photographer. "It's good he's covered with hair and beard. And the helmet. Come on; put it on. That's it. Pull it slightly over your eyes to give you a fiercer look . . ."

Then he saw Shishman. "Here's an example you should imitate," he said to Srbin. He turned to the leader of the company. "Just imagine if that one were our man. How beastly he looks! The Bulgarian soldier is a beast to the enemy! That's what he is!"

"He's an awfully bad soldier," said the corporal, remembering the incident with the empty rifle.

"It doesn't matter," said the photographer.

He finally decided to photograph Srbin in attack position. He found a spot, then ordered Srbin to assume a charging stance. The photographer set off to position his camera, but turned back when he was halfway there. He went toward the leader of the company and signaled him to step aside. "You know," he said, "it's me who's going to stand in front of him."

"You know best," said the leader of the company.

"Therefore," said the photographer, "it'll be much better if you tell him to unload the rifle. Just in case."

The officer thought for a moment, then called the corporal. "Tell him to unload his rifle," he said.

"Don't worry," said the corporal. "It's already empty."

The corporal gave the appropriate commands. Srbin's rifle was indeed empty. When everything was set, the photographer changed his mind once again. He asked Srbin to stand beside the trench so he could take a picture in profile. "If I take your picture head-on," he said, "it'll look as if we got the photo from the French."

The cousins could hardly wait to return to their spot above the rock where they could breathe in peace.

During the day many soldiers worked carefully to improve the trenches. They would raise the little pile of earth in front of each trench, fortify it with stones, and then cover the stones with earth. The very keen soldiers either smoothed the walls of the trenches or made hollows in them so that during times of attack a fighter could lie comfortably in an imagined position of defense. The cousins weren't interested in either activity. They worked only when they had to. Mostly they thought about Breznitsa, which was hidden from their sight behind Dolgi Ridge. Also, because it was nearer, they thought about Kolenovo and their Aunt Flora. No one ever saw them separated or heard them speak more than a few words. Therefore, they offended no one. It was clear they were frightened of everything, and fear is something every soldier respects.

When he made sure that no one could see or hear him, Srbin said, "Did you hear about Sunday?"

"About tomorrow?" asked Shishman, because the day was Saturday.

"About tomorrow," said Srbin. "They'll take us to church, the Church of the Holy Virgin in Kolenovo."

"All of us?"

"I don't think so," said Srbin.

They were silent for a long time. Then Srbin spoke with regret, "We aren't that lucky."

"I don't believe we are either," said Shishman.

The next day they realized that luck wasn't on their side. The corporals picked a few from every group. When their corporal passed through their trench, he grabbed Shishman by his sleeve to indicate he could go. But he didn't move. "What about my cousin?"

"Your cousin? Next time," said the corporal.

"Then I'll wait for the next time, too," Shishman said.

"It'll be a long wait," said the corporal as he released Shishman's sleeve. Then the corporal turned to another soldier in the line.

They were both sorry they didn't go. Now they looked toward Breznitsa even more eagerly and thought of Aunt Flora in Kolenovo even more intensely.

The night was filled with moonlight and the lake glittered like a mirror in which they might have been able to see their faces. That night the crickets were louder and clearer than ever. The day had been burning hot, and the sun had made the sky as red as an iron skillet. Srbin and Shishman hardly exchanged a word. They communicated with their eyes only, as they tried to suppress the longing in their hearts. Then on Tuesday morning Srbin turned suddenly to Shishman. He looked around to make sure nobody could hear him. Shishman heard him say, "I'll go to the leader of the company."

Shishman gaped at him. He didn't know what to say. Srbin got up, brushed his clothes, tidied himself a bit, and went off. Shishman stood silent and still, like a hare frightened he would be sniffed out by hounds in the hole in which he had found shelter. He sensed that if he stood up, he'd see something unusual on the other side of Dolgi Ridge. He didn't get up, in spite of his curiosity. Instead, his thoughts full of Breznitsa, he fixed his eyes on the trench through which Srbin would return. Finally, Srbin appeared with a bundle. Shishman didn't move. Srbin said nothing until he came closer to his cousin. He lowered his lips to Shishman's ear and looked all the way down the trench. "Follow me," he said and stepped backward.

"And . . . a pebble?" Shishman asked.

"You don't need a pebble now," said Srbin, and went on.

Shishman lifted himself out of his timidity and shuffled after him.

Bent and almost running through the trench, they came out into a little grove. They didn't look for a path. They kept going down, cut across the road to the monastery, rushed into the shallow river, and walked across it. They went uphill for a while and soon afterward they reached Kolenovo. When they entered the road where Aunt Flora's house was, dogs barked in the yard.

"Aunt Flora had no dogs," said Shishman.

"We weren't soldiers, either," said Srbin.

As they started to open the gate, the dogs rushed at them as they would after a wild animal. When the cousins persisted in entering the yard, the dogs attacked them as if they would tear them to pieces. Srbin dropped the bundle, which contained dirty clothes belonging to the leader of the company and the corporal. He took the rifle off his shoulder and began to protect himself with it, using it in the manner they had been taught for attack. Shishman did the same. But the dogs rushed toward them so fiercely that they had to flatten themselves by waving their rifles until Aunt Flora came out. As she chased the dogs away, she scolded them. "Shush! What the devil makes you bark your heads off?"

When the dogs had been coaxed to the back of the yard, Aunt Flora looked at the soldiers. She couldn't believe what she saw. She looked at them for several minutes, then opened her arms and said, almost as if she were singing, "My precious nephews! How foolish I am. I thought you were gypsies!"

Aunt Flora hugged them again and again, her eyes filled with tears. Soon Uncle Doné came out of the house. He was surprised as well. "I thought some beggars had come, but it turned out to be relatives," said Uncle Doné. He wore a rope belt over his long black sleeveless coat. He was wearing that same shabby hat he'd had for years and his mustache, as always, bristled. The dogs, seeing all this affection, wagged their tails, came nearer, and started sniffing the cousins' heels, knees, and army bags.

When they entered the kitchen, Aunt Flora said, "Take your shoes off, boys. Throw away those damn poles they've given you and sit down."

Aunt Flora walked back and forth through the house, fetching a snack and a drink of water for her nephews. Uncle Doné sat opposite them. "Tell us what happened. We sent you to Wallachia to earn money and now you come back as soldiers."

"We got ourselves caught on our way back," said Srbin.

"Didn't you think of escaping?" asked Uncle Doné.

"We did, but where could we go?" asked Srbin.

"It's easy to think about it," said Shishman.

"We spent a few days with Chakarvelika in Bitola, but she's on her own as well. Her husband left her and her son's in the army. She couldn't do anything for us," said Srbin.

"I see," said Uncle Doné. "Where are you stationed?"

"At the front here, above the village."

"It's not bad right now," said Uncle Doné. "There hasn't been any shooting lately. But who knows? Some time ago the shells ruined our fields, just before harvest. You're my blood and I hate to alarm you, but this spot is a glowing coal that will burst into flames again. They haven't yet finished dividing the world!"

Uncle Doné was silent for a few minutes. Then he rubbed his palms against his trousers, slapped his knee with his hand, and said, "Our job now is to save our necks. That's where we stand."

He waited for a reply from his nephews. When he heard nothing, he slapped his knee even more vigorously. "What do you say?" he asked.

"What can we say?" replied Srbin.

Shishman slumped on his stool, his head sunk between his shoulders.

"Have you nothing in mind?" asked Uncle Doné.

"Nothing yet," said Srbin.

"It's impossible, is it? The dirty dogs are watchful?"

"Ah," said Srbin. "It's easy to escape, but the Serbs will catch us on the other side."

"I suppose you're right," said Uncle Doné. "Now everything is so confusing. A long time ago when I was taken by the Turks, I ran away to the Montenegrins, Slavs like ourselves, and came to the sea. Later I made my way to Piraeus. I could go anywhere from there. 'Where do you want to go?' they asked me, 'to America or home?' And me, a fool, went back home. Those were different times. Yes indeed."

While Uncle Doné was talking, Aunt Flora set up a little wooden table before them. It was the same one she had put in front of them when they were boys. She began to cover it with food. First she put out a plateful of white cheese. Then the water jug, filled with fresh water. She carried in some grapes from the vines in the yard. She brought some of last year's walnuts down from the attic and put out some apples and pears. When she had finished, she said to Doné, "Go and fetch some logs to build up the fire."

"Very well," said Uncle Doné and got up. "But give us some brandy too. They're men now. Soldiers. Besides, it might help us to think."

As Aunt Flora tended to the fire in the hearth, she began to talk tenderly in her own way. "My dear boys . . . Last night I dreamt I was doing my chores. The hens, the pig . . . I was head over heels in a hurry, and Petra, my neighbor, got stuck on the gate like a blackberry bush. Every time I passed by to go in or out of the house she'd say, 'Mrs. Doné, Mrs. Doné, can't you see me here at your gate?'

" 'Oh, my God,' I said to myself. 'What's the matter with this woman?' When I woke up, I remembered the dream, but paid no attention to it. But now, since you two have come . . . I remember she had a brand new black headscarf on. The dream must have been a hint about you. It wasn't a bad omen. The scarf wasn't tied on her head, only placed on it, slightly askew. That's not bad . . ."

As she talked, she went back and forth—to the breadbox, the container filled with cheese, the cupboard. Then she left the brandy bottle on a little low table, and put the frying pan, into which she had dropped a spoonful of lard, over the fire in the hearth.

Shishman licked his lips and looked at Srbin. They smiled secretly because they knew that Aunt Flora would "conjure," as she used to say, peppers fried in flour with cheese and eggs. She didn't stop talking. "And your poor mothers don't know anything. If your wives could see you here in their dreams, they would fly over the moon to reach you. My poor hawks . . ."

Uncle Doné fed the fire with branches he had collected and broken up. When he sat down on the little stool at the round low table, Aunt Flora stopped talking. Uncle Doné opened his sleeveless woolen coat and adjusted his trousers. He stretched one leg along the side of the table and slapped the knee of the other. "Right," he said and lifted the brandy bottle. "For happiness and prosperity." He took a good sip while Srbin and Shishman watched him, their eyes open wide with envy. He passed the bottle to them. First to Shishman: "Go on, nephew."

Shishman took a sip and passed it over to Srbin. He sipped a little bit. Then he put the bottle down on the table, stiffened for a moment, and lifted the water jug over his shoulder. The water inside gurgled as if it were singing a song. The pleasant noise made Shishman thirsty, and after Srbin had finished, he drank noisily.

Uncle Doné stared hard at them. Finally he laughed and said, "Yes indeed. You are good boys."

Aunt Flora noticed his mocking tone. "Don't copy your uncle's faults," she said to her nephews. "There's nothing better in the world than home, with its water and its hearth. And your Uncle Doné, my dear boys, isn't someone to boast about. Since the village became empty, I can't keep him home."

"Eh," said Uncle Doné, as he lifted the bottle again. He drank, his body absorbing the liquid like a sponge. "Right," he said with satisfaction, as he put the bottle back on the table. Then he continued talking to his wife. "Put on a pot of water. Let the lads have a wash."

"Their Auntie hasn't forgotten a thing," she boasted.

Uncle Doné returned to the men's talk. "So, no escape for the time being. What about staying here, hidden? What do you say to that?"

"Noooooooo," said Srbin, dragging out the word. "It'll be enough if Auntie washes the officers' clothes for now. We'll see about later."

"All right. Agreed," said Uncle Doné. He slapped one knee. As he stretched out the other leg, he bent the first one. They said no more about the matter. For now Uncle Doné and Aunt Flora were the host and hostess, and the cousins were the guests. They ate the food Aunt Flora had put out for them, drank another jug of fresh water, and washed themselves under the porch. Then Aunt Flora filled one wooden dish with baked peppers and another with cheese. She wrapped ten roasted ears of corn in their husks and put everything in a parcel with some walnuts and some apples. Then it was time to say goodbye. "Have a safe journey. Share the little things I gave you with your companions so they will want you to come here again. As for the washing, bring a loaded horse if necessary. I don't want another soul to come to see us except you two. For your sake. Go now. We'll try to do something. I hope God will give you some luck."

Another visit was arranged—so they could bring more dirty clothes belonging to the officers. Then, again, Aunt Flora gave them a little something for their companions. "Eventually something will break," the cousins said to themselves. But for now they went back to the front, back to the trenches.

Every day was the same in the trenches. The cousins lived each day for itself. Once a week, if not more often,

they would go to Kolenovo, to Aunt Flora's. The corporal began to act more considerately toward them
because they took care of his washing and brought
back food. And despite their freedom, the cousins were
still obedient. Everyone thought the young Macedonians
were a bit strange, but nobody took them for fools, as
they had in the beginning. If they had gone away, the
company would have missed them. The first time they
had brought back food, they had shared it the best they
could, making no distinction between soldier and officer.
One day Ilija the Vlach approached them while they
were sitting crumpled against each other in the trench.
In one hand he held a tin box. It was the same kind as
Shishman's, the one the leader of the company had
thrown away. When he saw it, Shishman jumped onto
his feet. "Where did you find it?" he asked.

"This one's mine," said Ilija. "I keep my shaving
blades in it, but I have decided to give it to you. Would
you like it?"

"Eeee," said Shishman and his face melted with
gratitude. He took the tin box. The two of them were
so pleased with themselves they couldn't say a word.
They looked at each other and moved their heads from
side to side. When Ilija turned around and walked
away, Shishman sat down. "These people are good,"
he said.

"People are the same everywhere," said Srbin
thoughtfully.

Shishman looked for a pebble, put it in the tin box,
and shook it. The box rattled as his own used to do. "It
rattles just fine," said Shishman.

Life in the company was routine. With time, the
soldiers became more at ease with one another. The
leader of the company was intelligent, and he knew
how to overlook many things. He saved his scolding for

the worst offenders, and so the men took to him as they took to each other. Occasionally, they all got together to sing. Once they were determined to hear Macedonian songs, and so they called for Srbin, the one who was renamed Bugarin, God preserve him!

"I've never sung a song in my life," said Srbin.

But the men insisted and, as usual, the situation was a bit embarrassing. Then Shishman surprised everyone. "I'll sing you a song," he said.

They all burst into laughter. That didn't upset Shishman. He nestled his buttocks against the bare soil of the pit where all of them were sitting, laid his rifle in his lap, and began to sing,

"I once made a visit to Kostur . . ."

No one, before or after, has sung so beautifully. Thus, the cousins became known as The Macedonian and The Singer.

One day they were visited by some important officers covered with ribbons and medals. The officers, who had come for an inspection, went through the trenches. Some of them looked like giraffes as they peered over the top of the trenches and others were bent over, like cats looking for mice. They sneaked into the cave that housed the leader of the company, said whatever they had to say, and disappeared as quickly as they had appeared, back through the trenches.

The following day the leader of the company ordered half of his men to their posts and took the other half down to Kolenovo. There they called on the village mayor. He had collected axes from the villagers and gave one to each of the soldiers. Milan, the sergeant, signed for them and they set off along the path up toward the monastery to cut wood for fortifying the trenches.

They stopped to cut some wood on the path directly

beneath the monastery. Everyone picked out a tree to cut down, and the sergeant found a thick shade tree to lie under. Srbin and Shishman weren't in a hurry. Shishman waited for Srbin. Srbin waited for Shishman. Then, in order to find trees that would be easier to cut down, the cousins went higher up on the hill, above the others.

"Cut this one." Srbin pointed out a tree to Shishman and he himself went behind a beech tree where the ground was slightly sloping so that it was easy to swing an ax. So as not to appear too far behind the others, he assessed the tree with a glance, spat on the palms of his hands, and swung. The ax stuck in the tree trunk, and when he pulled on the handle to take it out, he noticed that the handle was loose. When he finally pulled the ax out of the tree, the ax head slid freely on the handle. "Damn it," he said to himself, then turned around to find a piece of wood he could use as a wedge and sat down to repair it. The corporal shouted at him from a distance. "Come on, Macedonian; what are you waiting for?"

"The head on my ax is loose, sir."

"Fraud!" somebody yelled, and the rest burst into laughter.

Srbin worked as quickly as he could. He didn't want anything to be held against him. After all, he was doing his job adequately. As he listened to the chopping sound of the axes in the woods, he thought he was in the mountains of Breznitsa, with his own people, gone in a group to fetch wood. That was the way they used to do it. When he finished the repair, he rose. He swung the ax once; he swung it twice, and on the third swing the ax sank deep into the tree trunk. The tree was rotten and hollow. Srbin spoke to Shishman: "Cousin, I'm finished."

He gave Shishman a roguish wink. He knew that

those who had laughed at him would feel outsmarted
and he was glad. While he was resting, he talked. "Comrades, friends . . . Run for your lives! I've finished!"

"Look at the Macedonian!" said someone.

"He's bragging," said another.

Srbin heard them laughing. "Never mind," he said to
himself and continued his warning. "Get out of the way
. . . everyone."

"Tut, tut," somebody said. "He started later than we
did and he's already finished. It's impossible! He must
be joking!" The laughter of the Bulgarian soldiers
echoed in the forest. At the same time, the dull thud of
the axes resounded.

"That's the way, lads," encouraged the sergeant from
where he was lying. "Bulgarian soldiers are capable of
laughter and good spirit both at work and at war."

Srbin stopped chopping for a moment and, because
the situation was serious, he addressed the sergeant.
"Sergeant, sir, I've really finished. My tree happens to
be rotten."

"What's the Macedonian saying?" asked the sergeant. "I don't understand a word."

"He's blabbering about something," said the corporal.

Everyone else thought the corporal was funny, but
Srbin was insulted. "So long as you don't say later that
you haven't been told," he cried out, as he swung the
ax once again. Once, twice, and the trunk groaned and
split open. "Tim . . . ber!" he cried, and ran back to
avoid being hit by the falling tree.

Everything happened in a split second. Srbin realized what had happened when a crowd gathered farther below to pull the soldier from under the trunk that
had crushed him. Poor man. It was that big mouth who
said he had come from Stara Planina, a village or town
somewhere in Bulgaria—God knows where. Somehow

they pulled him from under the tree, but the man was
already dead.

What were they to do? One minute the sergeant cast
a sad look at the dead man and another minute a sharp
look up at Srbin.

"I told you the tree was rotten," Srbin said over and
over, but in Macedonian.

"He did; he did," confirmed Shishman.

"You idiot! You should have said that in Bulgarian,"
said the corporal.

"I said it the way I knew how to," said Srbin. "Believe
me!"

"He did," Shishman said again.

"He said something . . . he did," said one of the
Bulgarians.

"He spoke in his own language," said Ilija, who had
given Shishman the tin box. "He didn't speak in Bulgarian, but in his own language."

The sergeant was totally confused, and so were a few
others. The majority, when they saw their companion
was dead, were furious at Srbin.

"The leader of the company will have to clear up this
mess," said the sergeant. He ordered his men to make
a stretcher.

Work stopped while they made the stretcher. Two
soldiers carried the dead man, and the others put their
rifles and their axes over their shoulders and got ready
to return to camp. On their way back to the trenches
the carriers changed shifts. Frightened and shaking,
Shishman kept bumping into Srbin, while Srbin tried,
as best he could, to keep his feet on the road.

When they reached the central area, dug out like a
lime pit, Shishman opened his tin box and put a pebble
in it. For a few minutes he held it in his hand so that it
wouldn't rattle. Then, while he stood close to Srbin in

front of the cave they called headquarters, he carefully put the box in his pocket.

The leader of the company was stunned by the sight before him.

"Sir," the sergeant began, "we have come back with one man dead before we could discharge our duty."

"I told them," said Srbin.

Without any explanation the leader of the company knew what had happened. He spoke calmly to the sergeant. "Did you explain to the soldiers how to protect themselves against accidents before you allowed them to begin?"

The sergeant was shocked by the unexpected question.

"I told them the tree was rotten," said Srbin.

This time the commanding officer was surprised. "What does that word mean?" he asked, astonished.

" 'Decayed,' sir," a few of the soldiers said together.

"We say 'rotten,' sir, in our language," said Srbin.

The leader of the company thought for a time. "Damn you all," he said. He walked nervously back and forth several moments with his hand on his back and his chin buried in his chest. Suddenly he stopped and gave the order. "Take the body to the village. Tell them there that a messenger with a report and a request regarding the disposition of the case will follow. The messenger may well arrive before you."

After he had spoken, the leader of the company withdrew into his cave. The sergeant immediately selected two men to carry the dead man and two others to serve as relief carriers. "Go!" he ordered. "The rest of you are dismissed."

The soldiers began to disappear into the trenches. Shishman stood rigid, with his hands in his pockets. Srbin looked at him inquisitively.

"The tin box," Shishman whispered. "Let's make sure it won't rattle."

Srbin put his hand in Shishman's pocket, took out the tin box very slowly, opened it, picked out the pebble, and returned the box to Shishman. Then they set off, Srbin in front and Shishman behind him. When they had reached their trench, they sat down next to each other, near their battle posts. Shishman would first look hard and steadily at Srbin and then stealthily shift his eyes to the left and then to the right to see if they were being watched.

A long time passed.

Srbin unhooked the little spade from his belt and began to dig in the dirt between his legs. Shishman stared at Srbin and at the strange activity he was engaged in. He knew his cousin was doing something important. For their own good. It didn't matter that Srbin's tree had killed the man. Shishman behaved as if he were equally responsible for the man's death. And Srbin had something in mind; that was obvious. There was a clear determination in his behavior. He continued digging in front of him until the hole was deep enough to contain his hand. While he removed the earth from the hole, he spoke to Shishman. "The tin box. Give it to me."

Although Shishman was agitated, he couldn't disobey. He took the tin box out of his pocket and gave it to his cousin. Srbin looked around to see whether they were being watched, then quickly placed it in the hole. He covered it with earth and buried it quickly. Then he got up, stamped the earth, smoothed it with his foot, went a few steps farther along and sat heavily on the ground. He began to dig another hole in the dirt between his legs. Shishman crawled closer and watched Srbin with even greater amazement.

"Dig!" said Srbin. "You dig as well."

Nervously, Shishman took his little spade and began
to dig in front of him. He dug so quickly that Srbin had
to reproach him. When the holes were finished, Srbin
began to fill them with earth. "You fill them up as
well," he said to his cousin.

They filled all the empty holes with earth, stamped
on them, smoothed their surfaces, and moved away.
They sat quietly then, the two of them, next to each
other, at the bottom of the trench, with their rifles
between their legs. Deep in thought, Srbin lowered his
head, while Shishman looked steadily at him.

The sun seemed to be stuck in the sky above them,
and the day seemed endless.

The sunset left a burning red trace and a shimmering
reflection on the surface of the lake. The valleys filled
with darkness, making the mountains appear soft. The
forms and shapes on the ground came to life as if they
were waking from a dream in a fairy tale. In the distance, the light along the horizon looked like an exit
from a cold, lifeless underworld where only darkness
reigned. Now the color of steel, the surface of the lake
made the growing darkness seem closer. The battle
lines were silhouetted against the sky. A long time
would pass before the soldiers would adjust to the
dark; then they would forget about the threat along the
horizon as they stared at the frightening shapes before
them.

Srbin, feeling like a sparrow in the translucent, secre-
tive night, and remembering the calculations of distance that he had made during the day, threw a pebble
toward Shishman. He heard it fall, then listened to the
silence. Srbin was worried. Shishman was supposed to
answer if he had heard the signal. But Srbin was afraid
that he wouldn't hear Shishman's answer. Something
might go wrong. Then all their plans would dissolve

and they might end up here forever, in this dark web of hatred. Tense with anticipation, Srbin could hear, or rather thought he could hear, a cracking. Time seemed stretched so far that he began to lose hope that he would hear any answer. He was already thinking of what to do when a flying object dug into the heap of protective earth in front of his trench. Relieved, he remembered that Shishman could hit a lizard right in the eye, and he was sure this was his answer. For the moment Srbin waited, as they had agreed. In the passing seconds, the darkness seemed filled with uncertainty.

Srbin threw a second pebble. It was almost the same size as the first had been. He threw it in the same direction, with the same motion. When he received the second answer and while he waited to throw the last pebble, he placed one foot into the hole in the trench that would serve as a brace in the event of an enemy attack.

He was no longer worried about Shishman. He knew that the minute his cousin heard the third pebble strike the earth, he would jump as if he had been released by a spring. The very minute he heard it fall. For a moment Srbin felt warm from fear that they might be making a mistake, but he didn't think very long about that. It only made him hurry to throw the third pebble toward Shishman. As he threw it, he jumped out of the trench with a force that could have knocked him unconscious.

Breathless, they found themselves together in a valley beneath the trenches. Frightened by their own presence, they ran down the valley as if they were moving toward an exit. Then they cut across the road that stretched along the lake, walked through some fields sodden with water, and crept into the blackberry bushes along the border of a field. Still breathless, they were unable to speak for a long time, and only kept looking at one another, wondering what they were going to hear if they spoke. The strain of being constantly on their guard soon forced them to move on, out of the blackberry bushes. They cut across one vineyard after another, terrified of running into French units. When the moon shone clearly, they felt safer in the shadows. They crept into the corner of a highly fenced vineyard.

The whole area glittered in a moonlight that made shapes appear naked, transformed, indefinite. The shadow that hid them was an island in a sea of uncertainty. They were silent, trying to identify forms with their eyes, trying to stay in touch with reality until morning came.

At dawn, they crawled out of their hiding place. They dashed across vineyard after vineyard, ran from bush to bush, from one field to another, until they reached a lane that forked off the main road and led up toward the villages. There they saw a huge tent surrounded by walnut trees. They crossed the road, cut across several small garden plots, and came nearer. They stood behind a stone wall, peeped cautiously over it, looked around them, but saw nothing. The tent looked abandoned, but they couldn't believe it was, because beside the tent there was a long table with chairs on both sides. Farther along, there was a large pot and other cooking utensils beside an open hearth. The whole place looked too well-organized to be deserted.

They brought out the squares of white cloth they had taken when they had decided to run away. They had escaped from the Bulgarians. The French army stood between them and their village, and their plan was to surrender to the French. Now they would really test their luck. They had never admitted it to each other, but both of them thought that after the immediate danger was past, they might find themselves at home, even tonight. Thus both were frightened but happy, impatiently happy.

"Come on," said Shishman, eager to cross over the next hill and to arrive home unexpected, as much for the sake of his family as for himself.

Srbin was convinced that there was still more to do. "Wait," he said. Frightened, with anticipation of the next inevitable step, he decided they should agree once more about their behavior at surrender. "Like this," said Srbin lifting his arms, a piece of the cloth in his right hand. "You lift both arms up and you say, 'We surrender! We surrender!' They'll understand, somehow."

Shishman stood with his legs apart, staring hard at his cousin. "Like this," he said, throwing up his arms and crying, "We surrender! We surr . . ."

"Don't shout!" cried Srbin.

Shishman, discouraged, and with an apologetic tone, softly repeated, "We surrender."

"Something like that," said Srbin, who began to look around as if he had forgotten something. After a few minutes he pulled himself together and spoke suddenly, with determination. "Let's go now."

They jumped over the wall and walked carefully, on tiptoe. They hoped to see a soldier, but in the morning silence they could hear only the twittering of an early bird. As they approached a walnut tree, Shishman stopped suddenly. "Hey," he said in a deep voice, and the sound thundered as if it were in a huge barrel.

Petrified, Srbin stopped and looked at him. Shishman said guiltily, "Wouldn't it have been better if we had walked with our hands up?" The "up" echoed.

Srbin's head sank between his shoulders. After thinking for a moment, he spoke. "You're right." He took out his piece of white cloth.

They walked on with their hands up. Following a

path beside the wall under the walnut tree, they headed straight for the table that stood between them and the tent. On the table were a few tin mugs and a big aluminum pot and ladle covered with a lid. The tent flaps were closed.

Thinking that the sentry was somewhere behind the tent and would appear at any minute, they waited for a time. The wait grew so long that Shishman rested his hands against the back of his neck, and Srbin felt his neck was as heavy as if he had been lifting millstones. Fatigue moved Srbin toward the table. Together they eased themselves past the table, approached the tent, walked around it and found themselves in front of the table again. Not a soul was anywhere. They walked away from the tent, but were unable to find any sign of life. Then they returned to the side of the table from which they had begun.

Far above them, the mountain ridge seemed whiter, in anticipation of the sunrise. Srbin wandered about. Then he signaled Shishman by putting his finger to his nose, and he set off toward the entrance to the tent. His heart in his mouth, he went nearer, then even nearer. With one finger, he pulled the tent flap aside and peeked in. Soldiers, lying about like recently slaughtered sheep, were fast asleep. Srbin returned to his cousin, his face filled with bewilderment. "They are asleep," he whispered.

Not knowing what to do next, Srbin sat down at the table in despair. He leaned on his elbows, resting his chin in his left hand and holding the back of his head with the palm of his right hand. Shishman continued rubbing the back of his neck. Abstractly, he gazed at the pot in front of him. First he touched it; then he began to rub it with his fingers until, finally, he held it in his two huge hands. He knew what he wanted to do, but was afraid of being reprimanded by Srbin. After hesitating as long as he could, which wasn't for long, he turned to Srbin. "Cousin! Can I look and see what's in the pot?"

The question brought Srbin out of his deep thought. "Take a look, but be careful," he said.

As he got up, Shishman lifted the lid and plunged his face into the pot. Still holding the lid above his head, he turned to Srbin. "It's either tea or coffee," he said.

Srbin said nothing.

"May I taste it?" Shishman asked.

"Go ahead," said Srbin indifferently.

Shishman carefully put the lid on the table, seized the big pot with both hands, and shook it to see if the liquid would go cloudy. "It's coffee," he said, surprised.

"Taste it to make sure," said Srbin. This time he was interested.

Shishman lifted the pot to his mouth and sipped the liquid carefully. He smacked his lips and stared at Srbin.

"It's not coffee," said Shishman, whose voice conveyed both delight and confusion.

"Is it good?" asked Srbin.

"It's sweet."

"What is it, then, if it's neither coffee nor tea?" asked Srbin.

After shrugging his shoulders at Srbin's question, Shishman lifted the pot again and began to drink without stopping. "It's *very* good," said Shishman, a smile spreading across his face. He didn't notice that Srbin was standing beside him, eager for a taste. Srbin almost wrenched the pot from Shishman's hands. "It certainly is good," said Srbin.

"It's excellent," said Shishman.

"But I don't know what it is," said Srbin.

"I don't know either," said Shishman.

During their discussion of the cocoa, a French sol-

dier dressed in a loose shirt and pants emerged from
the tent. As he walked, he stretched and gazed at the
sunshine flooding the fields. The mountain before them
was bathed in the sunshine of early autumn. The leaves
of the trees glittered scarlet. When he went behind the
tent to relieve himself, Srbin and Sishman stood up.

"He didn't see us," commented Shishman, terrified.

"I know," acknowledged Srbin as he moved away
from the table. They walked to the front of the tent. As
they faced each other, they began to lift up their hands.

"We'll surrender now," said Srbin.

They stood with their hands up as if they were posing
for a photograph and waited for the Frenchman to
return. Then Srbin remembered. "The white cloths,"
he said. They had left them on the table. They rushed
to the table, grabbed the cloths, and returned to resume
the posture of surrender. The Frenchman came back.
He was whistling as he buttoned his pants. The cousins, their arms raised, started to repeat the words they
had practiced. The Frenchman was still busy with his
pants. When he had finished and put one hand on his
stomach in a gesture of contentment, he raised his
head and saw the two Bulgarian soldiers.

"Mon Dieu!" he cried. For a few moments he seemed
to be under a spell.

The cousins broke the silence by rushing toward him
with their arms in the air repeating, "We surrender! We
surrender!"

The frightened Frenchman screamed and ran away.

There was a sudden commotion in the tent; then out
ran several half-dressed soldiers, some with rifles, others with helmets. Not knowing what was going on, they
began to run in different directions. The cousins kept
bumping into each other. They turned in every direction, but they were always together.

Finally, the French soldiers stood together at a distance from the two frightened enemy soldiers, who held tightly onto each other.

Then a man with bowed legs and a big head appeared from the crowd of soldiers. He approached the cousins silently, his face full of amazement. He spoke in their own language, "I can't believe it! You are Srbin and Shishman!"

"We are," said Srbin, dumbstruck. Even in his dreams he wouldn't have believed that they would run into Ljake, whom Shishman used to beat every time he could get hold of him.

"It's me. Ljake. Why do you look at me like that?"

"What on earth are you doing here?" asked Srbin.

"I'm an interpreter," boasted Ljake.

Shishman couldn't control his joy any longer. His whole being was touched. Stretching out his arms to embrace Ljake, he cried, "Ljake! Ljake!"

As Shishman was about to throw his arms around Ljake's neck, Ljake jumped back, threw out his chest, and cried, "Get back! Get away! Hands up! Just look at him!" he added a bit more softly when he saw Shishman stretching his arms upwards, the white cloth in one hand.

The French remained speechless until somebody remembered to ask Ljake what this was all about. Instead of telling them that all three of them were from the same village, Ljake said, *"Que voulez-vous que je leur demande?"*

A soldier with a mustache pushed his way to the front. *"Demande qui sont-ils et ce qu'ils veulent."*

"Who are you?" asked Ljake.

"Damn it, Ljake," said Shishman, annoyed.

"I'm asking you a question. Who are you?"

Srbin and Shishman looked at each other and then they shrugged their shoulders. Srbin spoke first. "I'm Srbin Vitanov, as you very well know, Ljake."

"And I'm Pero Shajkov," said Shishman.

Ljake translated. *"Monsieur le Capitaine, ils sont Serb et Pierre."*

"Qu'est-ce qu'ils veulent?" asked the captain.

"What do you want?" translated Ljake.

"We surrender," said Srbin.

As he looked at the crowd surrounding them, Shishman began to wave his white cloth.

"Ils se rendent, Monsieur le Capitaine," Ljake translated.

"De quel régiment êtes-vous?" asked the captain.

"What's your unit?"

"Fourth unit, fifty-third infantry regiment," said Srbin instinctively, as he stood at attention.

Ljake translated and the captain asked another question. *"Où sont leurs fusils?"*

"Where are your guns?"

"We left them behind. They're awkward for escaping with," said Srbin.

"Guns are like big sticks. To hell with them," said Shishman.

"They ran away without their guns," translated Ljake.

The captain thought for a while. Then he said something to his men, and two French soldiers ran to the tent in a great hurry. While the rest waited, Shishman asked a question. "Ljake, for Christ's sake, what are they going to do to us?"

"Hands up and keep your distance," said Ljake, as he placed his hands across his back and, assuming a position of importance, he twisted the top half of his body back and forth.

"Qu'est-ce qu'ils disent?" asked one of the soldiers.

"Des bêtises non officielles," said Ljake.

"Ljake," said Srbin. "In case of danger, remember to give us a warning. For the sake of those dearest to you."

Ljake didn't even deign to look at them. The captain asked, *"Et maintenant qu'est-ce qu'ils disent?"*

"Ils ont peur, Monsieur le Capitaine," said Ljake.

The two French soldiers returned, dressed in full uniform. There were bayonets on their rifles. They gripped the stocks of their guns with their hands as they led the prisoners toward the walnut tree. They ordered the cousins to sit on the wall while the soldiers stood on either side of them, their rifles balanced on their shoulders.

The other soldiers broke into small groups. They walked slowly back to the tent to begin the day according to their established routine. The cook, a bit removed from the prisoners, started a fire, then lifted the pot and carried it away somewhere behind the tent. After a few minutes he returned with the pot full of water and put it over the fire. While waiting for the water to boil, he kept a close watch on the prisoners. They looked at him as well. At one point, the cook winked at them and then got up to inspect his fire. Shishman and Srbin exchanged looks of surprise.

Always they searched for Ljake. Rage burned slowly in both of them. In a uniform, with a beret on his head, he had looked human. His legs, though, seemed more bowed than ever. It seemed clear that he had been testing them. He had pretended not to notice them. Full of arrogance, he had balanced on one misshapen leg one minute and then on the other, before one of them and then before the other. He had talked excessively, as though he himself were one of the French.

Then they spotted him, coming out of the tent with a book in his hands. He took a few paces forward, stood with his legs apart, and then lifted his head and stretched his neck. Because he was small, he looked like a cockerel on a rubbish heap. He even sounded like

one when he summoned one of the soldiers. "Etienne
Jouvé," called Ljake.

He closed his eyes and looked around, but Etienne
Jouvé didn't reply. Then, lifting himself on the tips of
his toes, Ljake called again. He glanced stealthily at the
prisoners to see whether they realized how important
he was. "Etienne Jouvé," shouted Ljake. "On the
double," he added, to impress the prisoners.

Etienne answered back, *"Me voici!"*

"Monsieur le Capitaine vous cherche," said Ljake
importantly, and retired into the tent. Etienne followed
him. The cousins could have beaten Ljake they were
so annoyed at him.

"Wait until I lay my hands on him!" said Shishman.
"I'll split him apart by his bowed legs."

"We're in his power," said Srbin.

"We certainly are!" Shishman confirmed.

"If only I knew what he had in store for us," said
Srbin.

Everyone had finished breakfast, but Ljake didn't
appear. After a while he came out and headed toward
the prisoners. He rocked back and forth on his bowed
legs and rested his hands on his hips. "Are you healthy
and well taken care of?"

"Thanks be to God," said Srbin.

They were quiet for a short while. Then Ljake spoke.
"I'm not doing too badly myself. What do you think?"

Srbin and Shishman looked at one another. Then
Shishman asked him, "For Christ's sake, how did you
learn the language?"

Ljake tapped his temple with his index finger. "Once
you've got a head and know how to use it, nothing is
difficult. Haven't I always said to you, 'I wish I had your
strength, but not your brains'?"

"Ljake . . . ," said Shishman.

"Let me tell you, Shishman," said Ljake. "Do you

see those two with the bayonets? One move, and they'll
rip your bowels open. This isn't Breznitsa where you
used to throw stones from the hill and not a bird could
fly through safely. Now your ass is in a crack, if you
pardon the expression."

"Times have certainly changed!" said Srbin.

"They certainly have!" said Ljake.

Although all three of them were calm, they appeared
to talk with hostility. They seemed to be spitting out
their guts with every word. Aware of his superior position, Ljake told them of his plan. "Let me ask you
something. You know I can help you considerably,
don't you? Good. You'll say I'm a loud mouth. But you
used to call me that anyway. Never mind. I boasted I
could beat both of you in a wrestling match. Let's
wrestle and you let me win. O.K., Shishman? How
about it?"

The cousins looked quickly at one another.

"Very well," said Shishman.

Satisfied, Ljake rubbed his hands together. "You'll
keep your word, won't you?" he asked.

"Don't worry," said Shishman.

Proudly, Ljake went to tell the French that the stron-
ger prisoner had talked him into a wrestling match.
While he was gone, Srbin asked Shishman, "Are you
going to let him win?"

"Hell, no!" said Shishman.

They waited without exchanging a word.

A group of men appeared. Ljake was in front, the
captain behind him with another five or six men.

"Amenez-les ici!" shouted Ljake to the guards from
a distance. "Come! Come nearer!" he yelled to the
cousins.

The cousins stood up. They set off with the guards
behind them. Both groups met in the middle of the
field.

"Et tu vas te battre avec celui-là?" asked the captain, pointing at Shishman.

"Bien sûr," said Ljake arrogantly. He began to roll up his sleeves. "Come on; what are you waiting for?"

"I'm ready," said Shishman.

"What about your belt and your canteen? If you're all dressed up like that, I won't be able to get a grip on you."

Shishman took off his belt, canteen and jacket while Ljake, his sleeves rolled above his elbows, danced before him.

"Come on, come on. Let me see you now," Ljake kept challenging.

"You attack me. You're supposed to throw me down," said Shishman calmly.

"Attack me if you can!" taunted Ljake. He was flattered by the ring of soldiers who had gathered around them. Then Shishman, despite his clumsiness, stepped forward heavily, opened his arms, and picked up the soft, flabby Ljake. Shishman squeezed him hard and poked his knuckles into his back. When Ljake's muscles relaxed, Shishman simply let go of him. The braggart dropped on the ground like the contents of a sack being emptied. When he felt himself free of Shishman's clutch, Ljake jumped to his feet and charged his opponent. "I'll show you . . . ," he said furiously.

The soldiers burst into laughter.

The captain understood the situation. He grabbed the arms of the raging interpreter just in time, and began to drag him toward the tent. Meanwhile the soldiers admired Shishman's strength. They ignored the interpreter and gathered around the prisoners. Some began to feel Shishman's muscles. The cousins would have made friends with the soldiers if the guards hadn't taken them back to their place under the walnut tree. When the incident was over, Srbin spoke to

Shishman. "I hope you didn't break his back as you did with that one in Wallachia."

"I didn't," said Shishman. "I only pinched him and he fell down. Don't you remember how big a softy Ljake is?"

"We'll suffer a bit because of this."

"I know," said Shishman.

Before lunch two soldiers brought out a table from the tent. The captain followed, with Ljake right on his heels. The captain stopped and looked around. The soldiers with the table waited a short distance away. Above the tent there was a willow grove, and before the grove a sloping field. The soldiers carried the table to the field and waited for the captain to show them where and how to place it. They put it at the edge of the grove. Then the soldiers went back to fetch a chair. They put that behind the table. Then they brought out the French flag and stuck its pole in the ground on the right side of the table. The captain inspected the situation and approved of it. In order to test it, he sat in the chair at the table, pondered for a while, and decided all was in order. He put Ljake in position at his left. Ljake stood and the captain sat down. He said something to the soldiers and they moved toward the prisoners. The cousins watched all this and waited. When the soldiers came to lead them away, they stepped forward. The cousins walked in front, with their heads bowed, the guards following behind them. When they reached the table, they all stopped. Then the captain remembered he needed someone to record the proceedings. *"Greffier!"* he ordered.

The notary clerk of the unit arrived with a chair, which he placed where the captain pointed, under the flag. He took out his pencil and waited, ready to take notes.

"Et bien, commençons!" said the captain. He ad-

dressed the prisoners. *"Nom, nom de famille, lieu et date de naissance . . . ."*

"Nationalité?" continued the captain.

"Nationality?" translated Ljake.

The cousins were confused. They looked at one another, but didn't know what to say. Srbin pleaded to Ljake, "Ljake, you know what we are."

"We, on this side of the front, are Serbs, but what you on the other side are, we don't know," said Ljake.

"Well, we are Serbs, too," said Shishman. "Let them write down we're Serbs."

"That's obvious from my name," said Srbin.

"You're lying," said Ljake, "but I'll translate whatever you say. I'm an official." He turned to the captain. *"Monsieur le Capitaine, ils se déclarent Serbes."*

The captain didn't find that peculiar, and Ljake, amazed, looked at the cousins.

"We're all the same kind of shit, Ljake. And that's a fact," said Srbin.

The interrogation turned to military matters. The captain warned, *"Il faut qu'ils disent la vérité, rien que la vérité!"*

"He says," said Ljake, "damn you if you lie. May eagles rip your flesh. May you be eaten by fish."

"We've nothing to hide," said Srbin.

"Not a thing," said Shishman.

Then, through Ljake, the captain asked them why they were surrrendering.

"Why not?" wondered Shishman.

"Wait!" said Srbin. "Why? Because we were on our way home from working abroad and we don't want to fight in a war!"

"Even if we had gone to war," said Shishman, "it wouldn't have been by choice."

"How many soldiers were there in your unit?" asked the captain.

"One hundred fifty-two," said Srbin.

"One hundred fifty-one," said Shishman. "You forgot about *him!*"

"He's theirs all the same," said Srbin.

"Who's that?" said Ljake.

"One fell ill," said Srbin, "but he might get better. Who knows?"

"It's hard to believe," said Shishman.

"What kinds of arms do they have?" asked the captain.

"Rifles," said Srbin. "And a small machine gun."

"What type?" asked the captain.

The cousins looked at each other and shrugged their shoulders.

"How are their trenches fortified?"

"Goodness!" said Srbin. "Since they've got nothing to do, they have difficulty keeping us busy. Yesterday we were cutting trees."

"What's the position of your unit?"

Srbin turned toward the battlefront, but couldn't see it. "How can we tell him?" he asked Shishman. He turned to the captain. "Above the lake, nearly all the way to the village, there's no army. Their position starts just above the village, all the way up to the top, where there's a cannon. The cannon marks the beginning of another unit."

"Where are the cannons situated?" asked the captain.

"There's only one—on the top of the hill. We haven't been any farther up than that, but the soldiers were saying that there was another cannon by those rocks up there, that it was the largest one on this side of the mountains, all the way to Igralishta. Above Breznitsa there were supposed to be another five cannons, but we couldn't tell exactly where they were." He turned to Ljake. "Do they need to know that?"

"Of course," said Ljake. "The French don't fight like other people. They only use pens, pencils, and instruments."

"I wish we'd known that," said Shishman.

"Have you told us all you know?" asked the captain.

"Tell him," said Srbin to Ljake, "we know more about what he dreams than we do about all those big cannons."

Ljake translated. The captain smiled contentedly and said the interrogation was over.

Then Srbin said, "For God's sake, ask him what's going to happen to us."

"Ils voudraient savoir ce qu'on va faire avec eux."

"On verra," said the captain. *"Nous attendons la réponse du quartier général."*

"We'll see," said Ljake.

They were taken back to their place under the walnut tree. The guards no longer stood, but sat on the stones behind them, with their rifles between their legs. It was dinner time. The cook brought food to all of them. He served the prisoners first, then the guards. The cook gave each one a plateful of army *cassoulet.* They even had seconds! And they drank lots of fresh water.

"I'm going to take a nap," Shishman said. He lay down on his side, put the palms of his hands together, rested his hands on a stone, lay his head against them and began to snore. He was dreaming about an immaculately dressed army. He, Shishman, was the captain. He was in command. The army was attacking the Bulgarians, with Shishman in front. They had no weapons, but they were dressed in shirts with their sleeves rolled up and they had pencils in their hands. They were attacking the trenches. Ljake easily captured the enemy soldiers and pulled their undershirts out of their trousers. He inspected the bottoms of the undershirts carefully, as if he expected to find something there. Then he took a pencil and drew a circle around each prisoner's navel. Afterward soldiers with bayonets came and pierced each prisoner at the mark. Later on, Shishman dreamt he lay in the trench, fast asleep. He was so sleepy that he was afraid the soldiers would pierce the marked prisoners too quickly. He said to himself, "I wish they could work more slowly so I could get some more sleep."

Then he woke up. His body felt broken and bruised from lying so long on the stones. He saw Srbin sleeping with his head resting on his knees. The guards were nowhere to be seen. Shishman was surprised, but he was also terrified. He nudged Srbin carefully. Srbin lifted his head, turned it toward his cousin, opened his eyes, and looked at him inquisitively. "They aren't here," said Shishman.

Srbin raised his eyes and, with a stealthy look, saw that the French soldiers were still around them. "Do you mean the guards? Aren't they still behind us?"

"No."

"Hmmm. There's no need for them to bother," said Srbin.

It was close to sunset. The cousins wondered what they should do—get up and exercise their legs, find someone to ask about their situation, or not move at all and keep out of trouble. Then, from behind, they heard Ljake's voice. "Get up if you want. Walk around a bit. Only here, among the soldiers . . ."

They were surprised to see Ljake sitting in the shade, his back against the wall behind them. He had a pile of willow branches beside him, which he was using to make a big basket.

"So you're still involved in gypsy work," commented Srbin.

"I am," said Ljake. "And why not? I make baskets, serve meals to *Monsieur le Capitaine,* and interpret for him. I do what I know how to do. And what can *you* do to justify your keep?"

The cousins exchanged looks. Srbin looked around and stood up. "Shall we talk to him?" he asked Shishman. "Damn it, aren't we the same kind, from the same village? Who's closer than the three of us?"

"Don't you mix me up with you too much," said Ljake.

The cousins decided to sit down beside him. As he sat, Srbin said, "Joke aside, Ljake, what's going to happen to us?"

"I'm not supposed to tell you," said Ljake. "Nobody knows. But bear one thing in mind. The removal of the guards means nothing. The most powerful organization in *La France* is espionage. The captain's interrogation . . ."

"So . . ."

"So, one doesn't know who's watching whom and why."

"I see," said Srbin and decided to make a mental note of something. "Fine! So, they do things cleverly— as you said."

"They use their brains," said Ljake.

"But let me ask you something else," said Srbin, without giving him time to prepare an answer. "Do you go to Breznitsa from time to time?"

"It's been far from my mind ever since *Monsieur le Capitaine* took me for an interpreter."

"It's right under your nose, Ljake," said Shishman.

"I've made up my mind. I'll go to *La France,* together with *l'armée française.* I'll work on *Monsieur le Capitaine's* estate. Be a boss. 'You,' he tells me, 'will only supervise and cut *les fleurs* and make *les bouquets.'*

I'll come back when I become my own boss, my own *personnage*."

"That's very nice," said Srbin. "And how are things in the village?"

"The same as ever," said Ljake.

"I'm sure you're right. But are they all well? How is everybody?"

"Your folks are fine. Nicho Lastagarkov died. When the Bulgarians withdrew, they took fifteen or sixteen people with them. Everyone who didn't hide or run away—like yourselves. As for the others, as soon as there's some more action at the front, they'll be under the authority of the Serbs. As you very well know, they'll find you no matter where you go."

"And our children, Borka and Pavle? They were very young when we left. How are they?"

"Spitting images of both of you," said Ljake. "The minute they began to walk, they went to the highest place in the village and stones began to fly nonstop. The village can't breathe in peace from your kind."

The cousins looked at one another as if they questioned his sanity. Ljake was still doing his job like a robot—quickly, efficiently, and expertly. That infuriated them. Not because they envied his success, but because he always did everything to show himself off. He was always perfect in everything. As long as they had known each other, Ljake had always been a thorn in their sides.

But Shishman was pleased with the family news he'd heard. "You say they're well—the children?"

"Little rascals," answered Ljake with authority.

The cousins realized that they couldn't trust Ljake. Now, particularly, they were nearly halfway between the front lines and Breznitsa. Several times they tried to find out information in an indirect way. They knew they couldn't expect any help from Ljake, but they couldn't stop building up their hopes when they knew that with a hop, skip, and a jump they could find themselves sitting around the table at home. Srbin began to question Ljake more indirectly.

"So you're about to go abroad."

"Yes, to France," Ljake said.

"And what about us?" asked Srbin.

"You? You're at God's mercy. As the old priest used to say, 'Each one carries his cross within himself.' "

Shishman's face was bloated with rage. His lips dropped and his eyes widened. "Look, Ljake," he said. "What if the other side grabs you? You couldn't get away. They'd chop a few inches off of you."

"More or less," said Srbin.

"Maybe so. But don't have a feast on my account when it's you who are laid on the table. You don't even know whether they'll stab you with a fork or simply throw you to the dogs. Ha! Am I right or not?"

For some reason, the cousins were not afraid of the worst that could happen. In a way this meeting with Ljake had relaxed them. They became talkative rather than withdrawn. They didn't admit it to each other, but they believed that the French would let them go now that they were so near home. They were moved to tears by the very thought.

Ljake came running out of the tent. He looked threatening as he approached the cousins. Shishman and Srbin, sitting on the ground under the big walnut tree, were just about to get up and wash their dinner dishes. Ljake slid toward them, his legs spread like a donkey's before a bridge. He waved his arms wildly, pointing at the tent.

Then he spoke. "What the devil made you come here? Get over there! Go to my commanding officer! They told him off! And all because of you! 'What do you

mean by keeping them here?' they asked *Monsieur.*
And we, the fools, were waiting for an answer! *Une*
réponse! And for whom? For nobodies! We wrote a
report, followed the guidelines. We sent it in the pre-
scribed way. *Prière de répondre.* What else could we do
but wait? *Attendre?* What are you waiting for? Get your
belongings. They'll take you somewhere."

"Where to?"

"To hell!"

"Ljake, don't have us on your conscience," pleaded
Shishman.

"Conscience or no conscience, this is *officiellement.*"

"Ljake," said Srbin, grabbing him by the sleeve. "I
don't understand your mumbo-jumbo. So tell me what's
going on."

Ljake moved away from him as if he were being
pestered by someone inferior to himself. Then he
rubbed his chin. He looked at the cousins from their
heads to their toes. Then he spoke. "Assholes! The
main thing is to be born with a silver spoon in your
mouth! I've been waiting here hoping with my heart
and soul, and now they'll be taking *you* to France!"
Ljake spoke enviously.

"Straight to France?" the cousins spoke in unison.

This was an opportunity for Ljake. "But of course.
You'll go by steamboat. It's waiting for you to set off.
Simpletons! Don't you know how one gets to France,
now that it's wartime? You'll cross seas. You might
travel for six months."

"Fantastic!" said Srbin, embittered.

"How far are we going just now?" asked Shishman,
weakly.

"Straight to headquarters. At Livadje."

"Are we setting off immediately?"

"Immediately. Absolutely," said Ljake. Then he

remembered that he had stayed longer than he should have and suddenly set off toward the tent.

All of a sudden Srbin ran after him and grabbed him by the sleeve. He looked at Ljake pleadingly and then spoke.

"Listen! Do us one little favor. Tell us how to say, 'Let us go to Breznitsa, sir, just to see our children' in French. We beseech you."

"What's that for?"

"No reason. Just to know. Your brain won't be impoverished by it."

"Aha," said Ljake. "Like this. Wait. This is easier: *Monsieur* . . . you know that word; that's first. Then: *Laissez* . . . Wait a minute. *Laissez-nous voir nos enfants.*"

"What about *Monsieur?*"

"That's the easiest part. Only don't put it in the middle. Either start or finish with *Monsieur.*"

"What about the rest?"

"*Laissez-nous voir nos enfants.*"

"*Laissez* . . . How did it go again?"

"*Nous voir nos enfants,*" Ljake spoke slowly and emphatically.

"I've got it, said Srbin. "*Nous voir. Laissez-nous voir.*"

"*Laissez-nous voir nos enfants.*"

"Wait. Not the whole thing. I'll never remember it all. I'll say what I've just said now and the rest is for my cousin."

"Me?" asked Shishman. "God forbid!"

The whole matter came to an end. Everyone was quiet for a while and then Srbin approached Ljake again. "Like this? *Monsieur, lai* . . . How did it go?"

"*Laissez-nous voir nos enfants.*"

"*Laissez-nous voir* . . . ," repeated Srbin and stalled again.

"Nos enfants."

"Nos enfants. Once more. *Laissez, Monsieur . . ."*

"Monsieur, laissez . . ."

"Mumbo-jumbo," said Srbin and gave the whole thing up. "Go on. Whatever happens . . ."

Ljake shrugged his shoulders and left.

Suddenly, overjoyed, Shishman said, *"Nous voir.* I remember that!"

"Only *Monsieur* is in my mind."

"Two words!" said Shishman. "That's something! If we tried harder, we could learn it."

"I know," said Srbin, and sat down on the stones.

Shishman dropped down next to him. They were silent as they waited to be taken away. They assumed that they would be taken first to Livadje, the headquarters. Two armed French soldiers came out of the tent, each carrying a bag over one shoulder and a bag in one hand. They motioned to the prisoners. The cousins got up and hurriedly set off toward their escorts.

As soon as they started to walk, the pebble in Shishman's canteen rattled.

The soldiers gave each of them a bag, and the others gathered around to see them off. Srbin and Shishman looked sadly around. In the eyes of the soldiers who knew that the prisoners were going to their country, there was a trace of envy. One offered his hand to Shishman. Then the two prisoners began to shake hands with everybody. Others came running. They kept shaking hands and saying something about sending their regards to *la Patrie.* There was no sign of Ljake. Srbin lifted his head and faced one of the escorts. *"Monsieur,"* he said, going through the motions of a handshake with his right hand, "Ljake, *Monsieur,"* he said.

"Laké," shouted the soldier.

"Laké! Laké!" all of them began to shout.

Ljake appeared, looking weak and exhausted. He approached the prisoners and stretched out his hand. "I had gotten used to you, damn you!" he said.

His eyes were filled with tears. Again the cousins shook hands with Ljake.

Then Shishman said, "And *Monsieur,* the captain!"

The soldiers, all in good spirits, called the captain. He came out and gave the soldiers a stern look. Then he shouted at them. "What is it? What's this noise for?"

"The prisoners want to say goodbye," they said.

The captain hesitated for a moment, but gave in. He approached the prisoners, first shaking hands with Srbin. Shishman held his hand longer while he spoke to Ljake. "Ljake, tell him we thought of him as our own father."

"Ils disent qu'ils vous aiment comme leur père, Monsieur," he translated.

That made everyone happy. The captain twirled his moustache, grinned contentedly, and patted Shishman's shoulder. *"Merci, merci,"* he said. *"Au revoir."*

"Arevoor," said Shishman.

They reached the main road and walked silently along it. Neither they nor the French had anything to say to one another. In the scorching heat their boots were slowly becoming heavier, their bodies sweaty. The pebble in Shishman's canteen rattled with a strange rhythm that was making one of the soldiers feel tired. Then he couldn't take any more of it. For a long while he watched the canteen dangling on Shishman's hip, but could think of nothing to say. Then, remembering that his own canteen was covered with canvas, he unhooked it from his belt, poured the water out, bent down, picked up a little stone, put it in the canteen, and shook it. The pebble inside rattled with a dull sound. Satisfied, he took two quick steps and grabbed Shishman by the belt. The soldier removed Shishman's canteen, hooked his own on Shishman's belt, and let go of him. Then, without a word, he grabbed his companion by the sleeve and allowed the prisoners to walk further ahead of them, so they would hear less of Shishman's clatter. Even so, they could still hear the rattling of the pebble. It irritated them, but not enough to make a fuss.

One Frenchman, eager for a distraction, began to tell his companion about the adventures of a friend of his at Antibes. The friend, it seems, was saying something to his companion in confidence about his wife, while somebody at the next table, without thinking, kept rattling his bunch of keys while he listened closely to a story his own companion was telling. As the French soldier continued to tell his story, the rattling in Shishman's canteen broke the line of his story arhythmically, but always when it was least convenient. He began to fear that he would either go crazy or that the rattling would spoil the pleasure of his storytelling at the moment of the punchline, when he related the unexpected fight that was supposed to provoke laughter. The dull rattle of the pebble in Shishman's canteen, although now somewhat muffled, was getting louder and louder in the Frenchman's ears.

Soon they approached the crossroads for Livadje and Breznitsa. The cousins, determined to go through their village at all costs, took the road to Breznitsa. Absorbed in their conversation, the Frenchmen followed them. The cousins were almost sure they had succeeded in this part of their effort. And they would have, if one of the Frenchmen hadn't managed to recover his sanity, which had been endangered by the constant rattling. The soldiers rushed after the prisoners. They grabbed the cousins by their arms and began to pull them back onto the right road. But the cousins dug their feet into the road and wouldn't move.

Srbin struggled as much as he dared, and Shishman wedged himself into the gravel like a piece of stone. The French shouted something that the cousins could only guess at. Without moving, they began to plead with their guards. The four spoke with signs and gestures for a long time. If the cousins gave in, their hope of seeing their village was ended. They decided to insist as long as they possibly could. Since their pleading was accompanied by a torrent of words, the French could do nothing but listen. For they were being outtalked and outwaved. The cousins argued with their arms and legs as well. They kept pointing toward Breznitsa. How near it was. Over there. It could be seen from the next bend. Out with their eyes if they lied! They were human. The soldiers should have some understanding. They had families at home. Mothers, fathers, wives, children. Young children. This big. As big as the canteen . . . almost. The old folks might be ill. Might be dying. And they might be dead by the time the cousins came back from where they were being taken—if they ever came back. After every few words Srbin would plead, "Please, *Monsieur* . . . small children, *Monsieur*. It's only down the road, *Monsieur*."

"For Arevoor, *Monsieur*," Shishman would sing out simultaneously. "Arevoor, *Monsieur*. Only for Arevoor. Cross my heart . . ."

The cousins were pleading with all their might, and more and more demonstratively, so that the French began to defend themselves. The cousins grabbed them by their hands, their arms, their shoulders; they dragged them toward the village and were about to start pushing them. They knew that the soldiers would understand and would feel uneasy about using force after their friendship. But, for their own reasons, the French couldn't give in. At the same moment one of them and then the other stepped back, grabbed hold of his rifle sling, stiffened, and peremptorily pointed at the road that led straight to Livadje. Reconciled to their fate, the cousins shrugged their shoulders and, like dogs with their tails between their legs, they began to walk, once again, in front.

They felt cheated and, even more, sad. After all that time, after having seen so much of the world, to be practically on the threshold of your own home and yet not see your own family! Who in Breznitsa would believe that they were a few steps away from home and couldn't even shout hello? But what can a man do? It was Fate, they decided. They walked in front of the soldiers, sorrowful, but hoping for a new opportunity.

As they walked, Shishman suddenly spoke loudly to himself. "I'll show him! He'll see!"

Srbin didn't reply. Sometimes Shishman would drop a single word, or he would loudly utter a section of a long monologue. They went on. After another fifty steps, Shishman asked, "Shall I tell him?"

Srbin didn't know what to suggest, although he understood that the question had something to do with him. He said nonchalantly, "Tell him."

He had lost hope of ever seeing his family. When his cousin stopped, he stopped too, to see what would happen. Shishman took hold of his belt and unhooked the canteen the Frenchman had given him. At the same moment the soldiers, wondering what was going on, approached them and stopped. Shishman offered the Frenchman the canteen. He offered it with one hand and asked for his own with the other hand. "To settle our differences, *Monsieur,* as befits the situation," said Shishman, angry and hurt.

The Frenchmen exchanged bewildered glances, but although the request was obvious, they seemed to understand nothing. Shishman persisted in his offer until the Frenchman, lifting one arm in confusion,

finally unhooked the canteen and gave it back to him.
When Shishman held his own canteen once more, he
shook the pebble out of the Frenchman's canteen and
handed it to him. Angrily, he turned his back on the
soldiers and, hooking his canteen to his belt, continued
walking with a hurt expression on his face. When they
were at a distance from the soldiers, Shishman, regret-
ting the event, said, "Did he expect me to lick his ass?"

They came to a bridge that crossed a dry stream.
Srbin and Shishman didn't go over the bridge, but
under it. Bewildered, the French wondered why they
avoided the bridge and thought, surely, it was because
of the pebble. Predictably, when they reached the middle of the parched stream, Shishman bent down and
picked up another pebble. But he didn't put it in the
canteen. The Frenchmen exchanged glances. Silently
they followed the cousins, watching what was going to
happen.

Srbin seemed surprised too, and he asked his cousin,
"The pebble . . . won't you put it in so it can rattle?"

"What for?" asked Shishman. "I won't . . . out of
spite!"

The French found themselves waiting impatiently
for the pebble to start rattling in Shishman's canteen.
They knew they had upset their prisoners by not grant-
ing their request to go through Breznitsa, but they were
afraid someone might see them there or that they would
be late arriving in Livadje. They felt so miserable that
they almost forgot why they hadn't granted the favor.
They imagined themselves in similar circumstances so
vividly that they couldn't help reproaching themselves.
Thus, they longed to hear Shishman's rattle, for it
would mean that he had stopped thinking about the
whole thing. All these thoughts were within them, min-
gling, mixing into different shapes as the impatient
soldiers strained to hear the rattling of the pebble.

Then one of them began to lose his patience and started to walk faster. He grabbed Shishman by his shoulder. *"Le caillou,"* he said. At the same time he pointed his finger at the canteen. He repeated the word, grabbed the canteen, and shook it. As soon as he understood the message, Shishman frowned. He snatched the canteen by its neck and moved away from the soldier. "Balls!" Shishman said, almost mocking him.

Srbin said nothing. From time to time he would look back to see what the French were doing. Since he didn't notice anything disturbing, he stopped paying attention after a while and, obviously buried in his own thoughts, he went on looking at his feet.

When they entered Dolneni, the village before Livadje, Shishman suddenly spoke. "Shall I put it in? What do you say?"

"Put it in," said Srbin and looked at the soldiers behind them. When they saw Srbin looking back, they craned their necks, but couldn't see exactly when Shishman dropped in the pebble. All of a sudden, they heard the rattling. Again Srbin turned his head to look at them. Shishman looked at nobody. He obstinately stiffened his neck and went on stamping his foot, the foot that moved the bouncing canteen.

The cousins felt as if they were entering Breznitsa. For them, Dolneni meant Aunt Sandra. Their grandmother, Trena, may she rest in peace, the mother of Srbin's father, had come from this village. Her daughter, Sandra, was married to Uncle Jolé, here in Dolneni. Uncle Jolé, they thought, might be fighting in the war, but Aunt Sandra should be here, and somehow they should be able to see her. They had no intention of begging the French to stop. Instead, Shishman stamped his left foot more firmly. Let everybody hear. Let everybody see that Auntie's little pets were coming. That's what their Auntie Sandra used to call them when they

visited her on St. Archangel's Day or on the Day of the
Virgin. When the visitors, the crowd from Breznitsa,
would enter the village, the children would run in front
and Auntie Sandra, since her house was here on the
road, would hear them from the balcony overlooking
the street where she would be waiting. As soon as she
heard Shishman's rattling, she would know that her
nephews were coming.

The pebble in Shishman's canteen rattled loudly as
they entered the village and approached Aunt Sandra's
house. The cousins were so overcome with anxiety,
they felt they were being lifted from the ground. They
thought they were restraining themselves from rushing, but in fact they were taking longer and more fre-
quent strides. The French realized nothing. They sped
up without being aware, but still the distance between
the two sets of men increased. The cousins began to
recognize the houses, the gates, the gardens. They
relived all their visits to the village, from the first to the
last one. Here was the excessively high gate of another
uncle, Uncle German, in whose house Shishman once
broke a water jug. To stop him from crying, a woman
had given him a whole box filled with wedding candies.
There, on the left, the little path that led to the
Makarovs. Down there lived that Krstin the crazy, as
she was known to everybody, who married Zojka from
Breznitsa. And here was the little balcony of Aunt
Sandra's house. But there was no sign of her.

There was no sign of anybody. No sign of Uncle Jolé
or the children, Milé and Tanche. In the fenceless yard
at the front of the house a few chickens were pecking
and scratching. "One of them is surely here; someone
will hear us, will see us, will give a shout," thought the
cousins. They were in front of the house when they
stopped, their mouths wide open. There were no glass
panes on any of the four windows, and straw pressed

against the bars from the inside. Then they noticed that the balcony was almost without a railing. Only a few bars were in place.

The French came to a stop behind them. They stared at the cousins and wondered what was going on. Shishman was the first to turn his eyes, big as coffee cups, pale with sorrow.

"Qu'est-ce que c'est?" the Frenchmen asked simultaneously. *"Qu'est-ce que c'est?"*

The cousins understood the question, but were so numbed at the sight before them that they couldn't think of a single word in their mother tongue. Their sad eyes stared, looking like the stagnant water of a pond. Unable to utter a word, they looked around. And when they didn't see anyone, they continued walking. They moved lifelessly and without hope. At the first rattle of the pebble, Shishman grabbed hold of the canteen as if to silence it. Now the sound seemed indecent. After a few more strides, he stopped and emptied the pebble into the palm of his hand. The French exchanged glances of amazement, but were unable to draw any conclusion.

All the way down to Aunt Sandra's house they had seen nobody. Now they searched desperately for a living person. It was the time of day when the men were still at work. It was the season for picking corn and beans, and for digging potatoes. It was harvest time. Therefore, they thought, they should meet people bringing loads home from the fields. They saw somebody up on a hill, driving a mule loaded with pack-baskets, but he was much too far away. From somewhere below a man appeared with a bundle of corn stalks. They decided to stop him. But they changed their minds when right after him another man, riding bareback on a donkey, appeared. When they were just about to speak to him, they saw a woman in the ditch below, with an iron pot balanced on her shoulder and wet clothes over her arm. She seemed to spring out of the earth and to arise before them. When she saw the two men strangely dressed in Bulgarian uniforms, but without their wide ammunition belts, and closely escorted by two French soldiers, she became frightened. She wanted to step back, to run away, until, suddenly, she recognized them. "For heaven's sake!" cried the woman. "Is that you?"

"It's us, Bozhana," replied Srbin. "What's happened to Aunt Sandra?" he asked immediately.

"Poor Auntie." Her voice sounded as though she were wailing for the dead in the graveyard. "I wouldn't wish her fate on my worst enemy. Her husband was beaten to death by the Serbs. He refused to serve in their army and she, poor thing . . . May God give mercy to her soul . . ." Bozhana felt a lump in her throat and began to cry. Then, wiping her eyes, she managed to utter softly, "She hanged herself."

"And the children?" asked Srbin.

"The children," said Bozhana, "are with your parents in Breznitsa."

While they were still talking, the man with the bundle of cornstalks came up, as well as the other man who was driving the heavily loaded mule. Other people came as well. The man with the cornstalks turned out to be a relative too, so he dropped his bundle on the road and came to shake hands with the cousins. The French began to feel restless. They understood nothing of the conversation, but as the people gathered around they were afraid of their own feelings for the two prisoners.

The villagers paid no attention to the French. Since the French could not understand anything, they were surprised when they saw Bozhana coming from somewhere with a full apron. She went to the French first and offered them pears from her apron—two pears for

each person. The man with the cornstalks brought out
a little flask filled with brandy from inside his woolen
vest and offered them a drink. He poured the rest of
the brandy into one of their canteens. German Markov
rushed home to fetch a full bottle of brandy. He poured
it equally into the French soldiers' canteens and encouraged them to take another drink.

All this put the soldiers in high spirits, but didn't
lessen their alertness. They didn't know what to do.
They knew that if they could understand the conversation, it would disarm them completely. As it was, only
a few curious villagers had gathered around them; the
majority—men, women, and children—surrounded the
cousins, now some distance from them. Still, they
didn't let the prisoners out of their sight, and when
they saw that they were heading somewhere, probably
into a house, one of them said loudly, *"Non! Non!"* He
waved his hand in the air.

The cousins faced the soldiers and looked at them.
Then Srbin said to Bozhana, "It's not possible, Auntie."

Bozhana, her eyes full of tears, straightened herself
up, retied her headscarf, wiped her mouth with her
hand, and stretched out her arms. First to Shishman.
She grabbed him by his head and kissed both his
cheeks and his forehead. She did the same with Srbin.
Then they all began to say their goodbyes.

Auntie Bozhana turned to the French. "You have a
safe journey, too," she said and kissed both of them on
their foreheads. Tears ran down her cheeks as she said,
"May my prayers protect my sons, and you as well, and
may God bring all of you back to me alive."

The emotional delivery of her words, even though
they could not understand what she was saying, made
such an impression on the French that they resumed
their journey to Livadje clearly moved. Indeed, the
gray, cool glitter of the lake below the road seemed to

contain the powerful emotions that all four soldiers felt as they marched aimlessly along.

Relations between the cousins and the French soldiers soon became less cordial. After they had walked for a while, they came to a small settlement containing a group of tents. The cousins looked around curiously and noticed that everybody there seemed preoccupied with his own business. They guessed that it was sort of a supply center. To them it seemed to be a kind of adults' playground, where everything was available. They were almost tempted to mingle with the crowds. Then they saw a tent a bit to the side, where, at the entrance, a few soldiers stood in a queue. The soldiers looked nervous and impatient; they seemed to be waiting to do something that made them uneasy. The cousins were puzzled.

When they had almost passed the settlement, their French escorts ordered them to stop. They looked back and saw that the soldiers were laughing. The taller one gave his gun and the equipment he was carrying to his companion and, still laughing, he went toward the tent that stood a bit to the side, and took his place in the queue. The cousins watched their guide curiously.

Then they saw a soldier come out of the tent laughing and buttoning his trousers. The cousins were ashamed. They were so ashamed that they were even afraid to look at each other. Nor could they look at the other soldier. Both simply turned toward the lake and stared at the glittering, but unmoving, surface. Slowly it absorbed the shame they felt.

Quite a long time passed before the tall soldier rejoined them and they were told to continue their journey. At first the French soldiers were noisy and the cousins felt uncomfortable. But after they had walked for a while, the soldiers became quiet. Only then did the cousins relax.

After a while Shishman suddenly said in a low voice, "He's probably not married!"

"Who isn't?" Srbin asked.

"That one," said Shishman, afraid to be more precise.

Srbin thought for a while. "He'd better not be," he said.

Shishman concluded the exchange. "God forbid!" he said.

They stopped to rest at Gropnarishta. The reflection of the sun setting into the lake almost blinded them. Side by side, the cousins sat close to the road while the Frenchmen sat just a bit above them. Then, so the difference between them wouldn't be pronounced, the French moved closer to the cousins, actually in line with them. The cousins thought the Frenchmen wanted their places, so they shifted their weight away from their escorts. Still, they were determined to hold their ground. Shishman unhooked his canteen from his belt and began to scrape its hollow side with his knife. First he drew a line across it and then he added a row of perpendicular lines on each side. It was a drawing of the battlefront from which they had come. Then, on one side he drew a few circles in a row and two that were slightly above the others. The two separate circles represented the two of them. Shishman planned to show the picture to his little boy when they returned home . . . God willing. "This is a picture of how I felt," he would say to the child, "when times were the most difficult for me." Then his son would understand. That's what Shishman would say to him.

"What is that?" asked Srbin.

"Nothing. A game," said Shishman.

The sun set behind Galichitsa, leaving a scarlet reflection in the sky and a darkness at the bottom of the lake. They stood up in order to resume their journey to Livadje. Just before dark they arrived.

This was their first visit to Livadje. The opportunity had come when they had least expected it. When they were growing up, they had always wished to go to Livadje in summer for the festival on St. Petka's Day. Both old and young used to go. The huge fair was attended by merchants and dealers from as far away as Kostur and Bitola. There were always a swarm of children and many beautiful young girls. People used to come for a day and talk about it for the rest of the year. After the time for the fair had passed, the cousins would yearn for the next one. But their parents, as if sworn to spite them, never let them go. "You're not stupid cattle like other people," they used to say. And now they were entering Livadje, not only without joy, but with a web of memories in their minds. Even as the web was being untangled, it seemed more and more intricate.

The soldiers led them into the yard of a house. The house was pretty, with an iron balcony painted blue; the courtyard, which was paved with flagstones, was round and the wall around it was made of stone and tile. The soldiers left them with the sentry in the yard and went into the house. As if not wanting to see something shameful, the cousins turned their backs on the door and looked over the courtyard, where the sun had already set and the sky was quickly darkening. It absorbed the rich color peculiar to the deepest parts of the lake. Soon, to their surprise, a third soldier appeared instead of the familiar two. He shouted something to them and pushed them toward a balcony on one side of the barn. Cautiously, they climbed the ladder and, from above, looked at the soldier who had sent them up there.

Despite the receding light, they found some bundles of cornstalks. Then they found a door and entered the section of the barn that was filled with straw. They hesitated for a while, but in the darkness they could think of nothing else to do but to lie down and go to sleep. They pulled out a sheaf of straw, bent it in half to serve as a pillow, and lay down. As soon as they had stretched out on the straw, feelings of pleasure filled their bodies. They settled down, and they heard no sound. Down in the stable neither horse nor bull moved about. From time to time they heard the sentry in the yard shift his weight from one leg to the other.

Twice the door handle creaked. Through the gaping barn door, they watched a lighted window and saw shadows moving about inside. But they were much too far away to hear anything. The cousins thought that the soldiers were probably plotting a conspiracy. They felt sadder and sadder.

Shishman spoke. "Sons of bitches! They didn't even say goodbye."

"Foreigners!" said Srbin.

When they heard somebody climbing the steps, they were afraid. Then they heard more noise. Someone was looking for something. Looking for them. They understood nothing, although they recognized the voices of their two escorts. Neither pair could see the other. All four of them were groping in the dark, trying to shake hands. The cousins were completely confused until the French finally managed to mutter, *"Au revoir."*

At first they had said something like "boomboom" which was supposed to mean that they were going back to the front. Now. Tonight. What luck! At least they had come to say goodbye. *"Au revoir,"* they said.

"Ah, arevoir," said Srbin. "Arevoir! Arevoir! Good health and luck to you."

"Arevoor, arevoor," said Shishman, as well.

The cousins went back to their straw and cornstalk beds. Over and over they asked themselves a question they couldn't answer. What burned so urgently under the Frenchmen's feet to make them want to go back to the front at night? They wondered about it, but knew it was none of their business. If they had thought about all kinds of things that weren't their business, they wouldn't have closed their eyes that night. As they lay there, the courtyard suddenly became lively. Steps became more rapid. There were sounds as if an anthill had come to life. People were shouting; some were crying out. Carts clattered on the stone surface of the road, like St. Ilija driving his cart across the heavens during a thunderstorm.

Once Srbin got up quietly and went to the door to find out what was happening. Shishman followed. The darkness was thick, and they could see little, but in the courtyard they could make out a large number of soldiers, some of them running from one place to another. They heard a chorus of voices in the courtyard, then nothing. Tired from their journey and their lack of understanding of the events, they became drowsy very quickly. "We don't know what's going to happen to us anyway," they said to each other. "At least we shouldn't be in need of sleep."

Shishman was the first to wake up from his dream. He was surprised to find himself on his hands and knees in the straw. Terrified, he whispered the name of his cousin. "Srbin!" Srbin jumped up immediately, and at early dawn they found themselves clinging to one another. Something horrible was happening, and still sleepy and caught by surprise, they understood neither where they were nor what was going on.

It was as if the earth was opening up and the sky was spitting fire, as if they were in the midst of a thunderstorm from which they could not escape. Shishman was already crying loudly and holding onto his cousin with the grip of a drowning man. In Shishman's painful clasp, Srbin began to get hold of himself. He realized the sound wasn't thunder, as he had first thought, but cannons roaring along the front. More than one was being fired at a time. First they felt the tremor under their feet. That was followed by a clap of thunder, which seemed to splash them like a cloud rolling along the ground. Then it rolled by and seemed to echo somewhere in the mountains behind them and under the lake.

Lured by the faint light of the early dawn, the cousins walked slowly onto the balcony. They stepped carefully toward the light, for they still thought perhaps the sound really was thunder. At the door they saw before them the glittering lake, just waking up. Toward the front, straight ahead of them, where the cannons roared, the horizon was clouded by smoke. At every new blast, new darkness sprang from the earth. In some places, fires flared from the soil.

Terrified, the cousins hid inside the door of the barn and waited. They noticed that the sentry in the yard was gone. That surprised them. They stared hard at the house for several minutes, but no one appeared. "They've gone," said Srbin to himself. All the French have gone there, into the flames, and forgotten about their prisoners. "Perhaps," he said to himself, trying hard to confirm his impression, "it's because there are only two of us." Still, he couldn't believe that things had turned out so well for them.

As suddenly as the cannon blasts had begun, they died out. Only a few belated thunderbolts were heard. Then there was silence. The cousins noticed that in the street, below the house and courtyard, a crowd of villagers had gathered. Stunned, they stared at the now quiet front.

Shishman looked at his cousin and waited to hear his decision concerning their future. Srbin fixed his eyes on the house to make sure that no French soldiers had remained behind, and the cousins caught themselves listening to fragments of the villagers' talk.

"A great power," one of the villagers said.

"The Bulgarians hid their tails between their legs," said another.

"Some softies those French were!" said a third.

"Ah," somebody said, "don't think that *they* are the heroes!"

"Who is, then?" asked another.

"The Africans! They are. Why do you think the French would drag the Africans here? To smell their color?"

"The donkey is invited to a wedding to carry the water," someone said.

"Don't jump to conclusions, folks! It's still uncertain who's going to win."

"It doesn't matter who wins. We lose."

The cousins wondered what to do. Srbin knew there must be some familiar faces among the villagers, but something held him back. He couldn't believe that the French had simply left them here, on their own, a couple of Bulgarian soldiers.

"I know," said Shishman. "Let's go down into the yard and pretend we're going to have a wash in the river."

After a long pause, Srbin replied, "And what if we step into a trap? What do you suggest then?"

Shishman didn't know.

The street was emptied of soldiers. Only villagers gathered at the far end. Srbin finally decided they should follow Shishman's suggestion. They went farther inside the barn and over to a trap door in the middle of the floor. When they lifted the door, they looked straight down into the stable below. They lay flat on their stomachs and stuck their heads into the hole to have a better look. Not a soul. On the side toward the street they saw a little window. When their eyes accommodated to the darkness, they could make out a door near the window, also on the street side. They climbed down into the stable and went to the door. Slowly, they removed the bolt and very carefully opened the door so it wouldn't squeak. One above the other, they stuck their heads out and saw the crowd of villagers, still standing at the end of the street and looking in the direction of the front.

The cousins decided not to come out immediately. Once more Srbin climbed up to the balcony to look for soldiers. He could see no danger. "We can come out," he finally announced.

The cousins had relatives in this village. They would go to them. The relatives would give them shelter and some clothes, and, with a bit of luck, the cousins thought they'd be able to go home. And if a Frenchman appeared? They would say they had only come out to talk to the villagers.

"And the pebble?" asked Shishman. He never forgot, whenever he experienced either joy or great fear, to ask Srbin whether he could put a pebble in the canteen so it could rattle while he was walking and share in his emotion.

"The pebble . . . ," said Srbin, hesitating. "Keep it handy, just in case, will you?"

"Very well," said Shishman.

He dug his hand into his trouser pocket, under his tunic. He felt the pebble and took it out. Content and secure, he looked at it for a moment. "Let's go now," he said.

"Come on," said Srbin, and they went into the street.

As soon as they were in the street, they became confused. Perhaps they had come out too quickly. They stopped suddenly, their feet frozen in place, and gazed at each other. How could they approach those people whose eyes were glued to the front and who didn't expect anyone unfamiliar to come upon them from behind? If they went near the villagers and spoke to them, they would seem like wolves entering a sheep pen. They stood and waited, but the people still stared at the nothingness. Nobody turned around—neither a man, nor a woman, nor a child. To stand behind their backs, in silence, was embarrassing.

While they were wondering what to do, the cousins noticed a little girl tugging at the single braid that hung below her mother's waist. The woman, like a mare chasing flies away with her tail, shook her head and waved her hand behind her, but the little girl kept pestering her. Only when the woman turned around to grasp the girl by her shoulders did she see the two Bulgarian soldiers. She suddenly realized that she had seen something peculiar, and she turned white with fright. She cried out, horrified, "Good God! Fortune has dealt us another blow!"

Startled, the people turned toward her and saw the two disheveled, heavily bearded Bulgarian soldiers standing there. The woman was already fleeing with the little girl in her arms.

"The Bulgarians!" someone said, and the others, still staring, began to walk backward, ready to break into a run. In their terror, they didn't notice that there were only two of them—ordinary, unarmed, and unkempt.

After a moment Srbin called out, "Brothers! Hey! We're from Breznitsa!"

"Friends!" Shishman called after them.

The crowd hesitated in their retreat. With their arms outstretched, the cousins came nearer, step by step, their faces pleading. The people stood in disbelief. Because of their overgrown beards, nobody could recognize who they were.

"Who are you?" It was lucky someone asked as he bravely took one step toward them.

The people stood waiting to see what was going to happen.

"From Breznitsa! We're runaways from the Bulgarians! From the front . . ." said Srbin. "I'm Srbin. Srbin . . ."

"I'm Shishman," Shishman said for himself.

"Grozdan's grandsons," said the villagers.

"Grozdan's," repeated Shishman.

Then the villagers gathered around them. They shook their heads and gave them their sympathy, wondering what to ask them, if, indeed, they should ask them anything at all. They were certain the cousins weren't lying.

A big bearded man, all in rags, who looked like a giant stuffed bird, pushed his way forward. He stretched out his hand to welcome them and said, "I'm your closest relative here in the village. I'm Koté Maljanov. An uncle, if you can remember me," he said.

"Uncle Koté!" Srbin said.

"That's right," said Koté. "We've lost track of each other because of poverty and hard times. You know me from Medovo, but I moved here when my wife's mother died. I had nothing there anyway."

Shishman wasn't listening to any of it. Convinced that the time had come to be calm and relaxed, he took hold of his canteen, dropped into it the pebble that he had been squeezing between his thumb and index finger, and rattled it. As he rattled it again, he said to the canteen, "We haven't been without luck! Believe me!"

Their rediscovered uncle looked at the people and spoke, "Listen, friends . . ." and then he paused to check whether they were listening carefully. "As Srbin and Shishman's closest relative, whether I want it or not, whether I can afford it or not, I'll take them to my house. I'll feed them and help them find different clothes. And you—you've neither heard nor seen anything. Let's make that clear!"

"We'll mind our own business," said somebody. "If the French have made a break for it, we won't see any more of them. Rest assured, as far as they are concerned, for they've got homes and families in their own country. They have had enough of the past three years without wasting their time here. The one to beware of is the Greek. As you know, the mayor of this village waits, twirling his mustache, anxious for his turn to boss us about."

"That's my problem," said Koté.

By noon it was already clear that the front had finally been broken and the violence had dissolved.

They were sitting in front of the fire in Koté Maljanov's kitchen having breakfast—Koté and the cousins, Srbin and Shishman. Koté's wife took out a pot filled with beans she had been warming up, poured some out into a big earthenware bowl, and put it before the three men. She brought out three wooden spoons and gave them each one. From the breadbox on the other side of the sink, she took a loaf of bread and handed it to her middle daughter, Mara, to serve. Koté took the bread and tore a piece for each man. He gave the rest back to Mara, and then the three men dug into the beans, holding the bread in one hand and the spoon in the other. The cousins ate hungrily. Between bites, speaking with difficulty, Shishman said, "Honestly, Uncle, we've crossed many a border, but there isn't food like this anywhere! If there isn't food to eat with a spoon, forget it!"

"Do you want some hot peppers?" asked Koté's wife, standing by the sink.

"That would be nice," said Srbin.

"Yes, yes," added Shishman eagerly. "If you have a dried pepper to grill over the fire . . . One from last year."

Morning light began to stream through the two window panes not stuffed with rags, accentuating their dirtiness and the smokiness of the room. Koté lifted his head toward the window and addressed his wife. "Woman, send the girls to the field to dig potatoes. What do you plan to do today?"

"If you don't need me," Koté's wife replied, "I'll go with them."

"Go," said Koté. "As soon as we finish eating, we'll try to think of some way these boys can get home. Then we'll go to Vrkikot to cut the cornstalks."

"Don't worry too much about us, Uncle," said Shishman. "Just tell us how we can help you while we're here. It's easy for us now! I've only got one problem."

"What's your problem, son?"

"The canteen was perfect," said Shishman, "but it's awkward for a civilian to carry. Do you have any ideas?" He turned to Srbin.

"Uncle, do you have a tin box of some kind? One that held shoe polish, or something similar? An empty one?" asked Srbin.

"A tin box?" asked Koté in amazement. "What for?"

"I've got a bad habit," said Shishman. "That's why."

"What kind of a bad habit can you have? You, who are fit as a fiddle, a bull of a man?" asked Koté.

"He's joking, Uncle," said Srbin. "He needs a box to keep a pebble in. He's set in his mind and heart to take it to his children."

"Why didn't you say so?" asked Koté. "I was worried for a moment. Look for a tin box, woman!"

All this time Koté's wife had been watching them with disbelief. Now, distracted by her own thoughts, she said, "I still don't know what kind of a box you want, but I'll see what I can find."

"Bring whatever you can find," said Shishman, "and I'll tell you whether it will do. A shoe polish container would be best, if you have one."

"Hardly," said Koté's wife. "One needs to wear shoes in order to need shoe polish. But I'll take a look."

Koté's wife went out to look around the house for something that would be suitable, and Koté took out his tobacco pouch and his pipe. He began to fill the pipe, saying, "It's difficult to find things like a tin box in a house without sons."

Just as Koté was lighting his pipe with a little branch from the fire, a shadow crossed the window. The shadow stopped, then cried out, "Koté! Are you in?"

"Who's that?" asked Koté. "Come in. You're not an enemy."

Then the door clicked. The visitor shuffled behind the door to leave his walking stick and came into the kitchen. Unshaven like the other men, the thinness of his face and body were hardly noticeable.

"Good morning," said the man, as he rubbed his hands in front of himself and looked around as if searching for something.

"Good morning, Metodija," said Koté. "Come on; grab a chair. Sit down and tell us what good news brings you here."

"Well," said Metodija, taking a little stool and moving toward the warmth of the fire. "If I had been born lucky, I wouldn't have been a serf in a family of serfs."

"Come on, come on. Don't give me the creeps. Speak your business."

Metodija settled down, stretched his hands over the fire, and with his eyes focused on the hearth, he said, "The mayor."

"What about him?" asked Koté. "He's begun his shitty talk, has he?"

"Yes," said Metodija. "He pretends to be all innocence, but he's filled with the slyness of a Greek. He's the mayor and all this area will be Greek. Get it?"

"I get it all right, but what's that got to do with me?"

"Because of your nephews," said Metodija.

"What about my nephews?"

"Now you're making me sell you brains. Our village has spies everywhere. You hadn't even shaken hands with the boys and already he knew more than you did."

"Listen, you!" shouted Koté. Then he thought for a second. "Doesn't he know that a man lives with other men?"

"That Vlach is cunning," said Metodija. "Do you remember when he came to this village with only a bag in his hands? He was mending shoes made from pig's leather and now he has a grand house, an estate. He's even trading in Salonica! The Greeks planted him when the French were here. He was to serve them as the civilian leader while they fought their war. But what's to be done? He's the master and I, as you know very well, am a serf in his house."

"And an informant as well," said Koté.

"Don't you mock me," reproached Metodija. "I've been talking to you as a friend. 'Listen to me,' he says. 'When your turn comes, you'll be a policeman; you'll live on a salary.' What else can I do?"

"I'm not talking about that. Just don't make strangers of your own people, I tell you."

"Koté," Metodija acknowledged, "nothing is certain. A poor man can be in anybody's harness."

The cousins listened carefully and exchanged occasional glances. Shishman, slightly agitated, had opened the right side of his homespun coat and was searching for something inside. He eased his hand inside and covered it with the front of the coat. He wasn't sure what Metodija was up to. Srbin pretended he wasn't looking or even listening.

Koté asked Metodija, "And what's the trouble now?"

"Nothing," said Metodija. "He's asking you to come and talk with him. All of you together."

"What can I do? There isn't one," said Koté's wife, still outside. When she saw that there was another guest, she stood motionless. Then she recognized him. "Is that you, Metodija? What luck brings you here?"

"I came to warm myself a bit," said Metodija.

"You're very welcome," said Koté's wife. "How is everybody at your house? How are they doing?"

"Very well, thank you," said Metodija.

"Go, woman, if you still intend to," said Koté.

"Don't you need me?" asked Koté's wife.

"No," said Koté.

"But what about that damned box, lads?"

"Forget it, forget it," said Srbin as he gave Shishman a reassuring look, for his cousin had seemed worried.

"I'll be off, then," said Koté's wife.

After a few attempts, Koté managed to light his pipe. Later, he tapped the bowl on a log to empty it, took a knife out of his pocket and scraped the inside of the pipe. Then he put the pipe inside the pocket of his jacket. Next, he pulled the logs out of the fire and put out the fire by rubbing the logs together. He stood them vertically, with the burned ends pointing up, and spread

out the ashes with the tongs. After that, he tightened
his pig-leather shoes. Metodija and the cousins watched
him in silence because they knew he was trying to
decide what he should say.

He looked straight into Metodija's eyes. Then he
said, "Listen. Today I had planned to cut the cornstalks and dig up the potatoes. I wanted to bring them
here and then sort them in the barn. Would it be a
problem if I finished my work first?"

"Koté," said Metodija, shrugging his shoulders. "I
don't think so, but how can I say anything and be
sure?"

"Right. I thought you couldn't," said Koté. "Therefore, get up, boys, and let's go." He stood up. Metodija
and Srbin followed. Shishman lifted his head pleadingly and searched his cousin's eyes. Srbin knew what
he had on his mind.

"Come on, what's keeping you?" Koté said impatiently.

"Uncle," said Srbin, "The canteen. Where is it?"

"Why do you need the canteen?" Koté, who wanted
it for himself, was annoyed.

"Just for a while. Until we find a proper box."

"Hmmm," said Koté, losing his temper. "How do I
know where the wife has put it?" He went outside. Not
wanting to get involved, Metodija stared at the door
and silently tried to figure out the issue over the canteen. Fortunately Koté found the canteen and came
back inside. He almost threw it at the cousins. Shishman
seized it and hooked it quickly onto the narrow belt
under his homespun coat. As if he were alone, he
adjusted it, then checked to see what it looked like
under the coat. As he pushed his hand into his pocket,
he asked, Srbin, "Shall I put it in?"

"Maybe there isn't any need," said Srbin.

Neither Koté nor Metodija understood a thing. More

from consternation than respect, they let the cousins go out the door first. Then they exchanged glances and, as Koté reached for the key to the front door, Metodija went out before him.

The mayor of the village was on his balcony, cutting leather to make shoes. From his high perch, he saw Metodija coming with three companions into his yard. He picked up another piece of leather and began to cut it. He evened one side and trimmed it as near the end as he could. Then he spread it on the floor and, taking a piece already cut for a pattern, he began to measure and to mark the leather with a knife. He didn't even turn toward his visitors to greet them. He looked very busy with the measuring. The four men gathered around him and watched him measure and mark, slowly and carefully. When he had finished, he said, "Now I must cut them apart." He looked at Koté and quickly eyed the cousins. With the piece of leather in his hands, he moved toward Shishman and thrust it at him. "Hold it. You can help me finish the job." He spoke with an accent characteristic of the Vlachs, an accent that reminded the cousins of the Vlach dialect they had heard in the small mountain dairies around Breznitsa.

Shishman didn't move. He looked at Srbin. Srbin wrinkled his forehead and hurriedly withdrew his eyes. Then Shishman, with his head turned away from the job, stretched his arms out slowly. The mayor roughly pushed the leather into his hands. When he felt it, Shishman pressed his thumbs and index fingers together. As the mayor began to flick his knife between Shishman's belly and the piece of leather, Shishman concentrated hard on his work. The mayor cut quickly and skillfully. He grabbed hold of the leather, then slung it into Shishman's hands. He flicked the knife again, stretching his hand as if he were going to stab

Shishman in the stomach from underneath. That terrified Shishman, and he felt his stomach churning. He
thought he couldn't endure another round. Fortunately
the Vlach had finished. He picked up the pieces, and
put them in the pile with the others. Then he unfas-
tened his apron, wiped his hands on it, and threw it on
top of the waste pieces. As he stood upright before
them, they could see he was tall and slightly stooped.
He had a hooked nose, thin lips, and a long face. He
spoke at a pace that was much faster than his mouth
could handle, so it sounded as if he had a slight stutter.
After looking at the four men before him for a moment,
he put his hands on his hips as if he were trying to
straighten himself. He offered to shake hands with
Koté and then with the cousins, who were cordial, but
reserved.

"Welcome . . . I'm sure you're as busy as I am; but
that's life. Come in, come in. We're all human." He
entered before them, his strong Vlach accent ringing
in the cousins' ears.

The room was clean and painted white. On first
impression it was a pleasant room. The window panes
shone and were framed with curtains. Between the
door and the hearth, there was a rag carpet. A trunk,
covered with a gaily patterned cotton cloth, sat next to
the hearth and under the window. In the opposite
corner stood a large rectangular table with a bench on
each side and a chair at its head. The Vlach led them
straight to the table. He went immediately to the head
and stood while he pointed out to each one where he
should sit. Then he sat himself. Everyone, except
Metodija, who was waiting for directions, sat down.
The mayor spoke first to him. "Go, Metodija, and tell
the women to make us some coffee."

Metodija left and didn't return immediately. Then
the mayor turned to Koté. "Koté, don't be angry with

me. You know . . . ," he placed the palm of his hand over his heart, "that my first concern is the village. And the authorities have an eye on me."

"What if the Serbs or Bulgarians come?" asked Koté.

"I count on my luck, Koté, but I count on my friends as well. Like you. If you hear something, you tell me about it. My fate is obvious. I would have to flee before them as fast as I could."

"So. You're sure the Greeks are coming here?" asked Koté.

"Koté," said the mayor, "it is necessary to protect yourself from both sides."

"Wait a minute now," said Koté. "Did you call my nephews here because you suppose Breznitsa will also be under the control of the Greeks?"

"I don't know, Koté," said the mayor, as he straightened up. "I called them here in order to protect myself. Tomorrow the Greeks will come. If they hear about your nephews, I'll be finished. And you will too!"

"What can be done?" asked Koté.

"That's why I called you here. To discuss things. To 'open the book' and see."

"Come on, then, 'open the book,' " said Koté.

Leaning on the table with both hands, the old man looked hard at the cousins. He was about to take a quick breath before he asked them whatever he was going to ask. But at that moment the door handle clicked and an old woman with a tray in her hands entered the room. She left the tray on a little chair near the door and came to the table to welcome the guests. She was the mayor's mother. Stooped and dressed like a Vlach, with her head tied in a white scarf, she looked like her son. But her lips were blue and somewhat droopy. After shaking hands with the men, she put the coffee on the table and left the room.

The mayor changed the subject of the conversation.

While they were drinking their coffee he said nothing about the cousins. He asked Koté about his work, his household, his family. "How are your daughters?"

"Fine, thanks," said Koté, as if he had been wounded slightly.

"Koté, you don't realize your wealth," the mayor said. "If I had three daughters like yours, I wouldn't care who came into power."

"Don't tell me that," said Koté. "Who expects any good from a woman?"

"Don't tell me it's been hard for you living off your wife's wealth. I'll talk to you another time—if we still remain friends."

As they finished their coffee, he said, "To your health" to each guest and then put the cups on the tray. Then he put his hands on the table again and looked once more at the cousins. "You're from Breznitsa, aren't you?" he asked.

"From Breznitsa," said Srbin.

Shishman nodded his head affirmatively.

"Good," said the mayor. "And what are you?"

"Christians," said Srbin.

The mayor smiled. "I didn't mean that. I meant 'what are you?' in another way."

"In what way?" asked Srbin and he began to think. Shishman looked at him impatiently as he waited to hear what Srbin was going to say. Like a rabbit in a hole, Srbin continued to stall. "In that way . . . in that way, we're Macedonians," he said.

The mayor began to shake his head. He threw up his arms in dismay. Then he looked at Koté as if he were wondering what he could do with these men who didn't help him so he could help them. "You're still novices," he said. "Don't you see, Koté, what would have happened if I weren't your friend?"

"What are they, then?" asked Koté.

"Koté, Koté," said the mayor as he left his seat. All three of them watched him breathlessly. The mayor went to the trunk under the window. He dipped his hand into his baggy pants, behind the braided decoration that marked the pocket. His arm disappeared inside, almost up to his elbow. Then he withdrew it and produced a key. He unlocked the padlock on the trunk, and with another key he unlocked the trunk lock and lifted the lid. He took out a huge notebook. Then he closed the lid and returned to the table. He placed the notebook in front of him and opened it.

"So you're from Breznitsa," he said. "From Breznitsa . . . from Breznitsa . . . ," he kept repeating as he turned the pages. He slid his index finger from the top to the bottom of every page and then turned the page. Finally he said, "From Breznitsa. Here. *Village of Breznitsa,*" he read in Greek. "The priest there is *Hristo Hristomanos, Elenikos.* That means that you're Greek. It all depends on the nationality of your village priest."

The cousins looked at each other. They remembered that nobody in the village could understand the language the priest spoke in church; he sang in a funny language, the villagers used to say. The priest was from Breznitsa, but he had been educated in Greece, in Greek. On the cousins' faces there was a look of amazement, but of enlightenment as well, since they'd finally discovered why the priest was so important.

"That's right," said Srbin.

"That's right," Shishman repeated.

"Do you see now?" asked the mayor, exulting.

"So we're Greek," said Shishman. "That's that."

"An archer is not known by his arrows, but by his aim," said Srbin. "It's written there—in black and white."

"That's right," said the mayor.

"So," interrupted Koté, "they can mind their own

business." He began to think more and more about the cornstalks and the potatoes.

"Wait a minute. Don't be in too big a hurry, Koté," the mayor warned him.

"What do you mean?" asked Koté. All of a sudden he was confused and didn't know what to say.

"I'll tell you," said the mayor. "Let's say they set off to go home, to Breznitsa. Fine. And the Greeks will set off from Florina to come there too. Now let's suppose they meet. Can you see the spot your nephews could find themselves in?"

"Yes, I can," said Koté, stroking his beard. "What's the solution?"

"I'll tell you, so you'll realize you're among friends," the mayor said as he turned to the cousins. "When do you intend to go home?"

"I intend to get them out of the village tonight," said Koté.

"That's wise," said the mayor. "I'll write a letter of permission for them. Such and such men. Greeks, from such and such place. Going home. Sealed, signed, everything."

"Write, then," said Koté.

"Write?" asked the mayor, amazed. "let me see you sit right down and do it!"

"I know nothing about that kind of shit."

"Ah," said the mayor. His voice seemed to drag. "You see, writing is not the same as digging. It needs thinking, style. Such needs demand time!"

"When do you want us to come back, then?" asked Koté.

"Well," said the mayor, "I know you've got work to do, the crop to harvest. I won't waste your time. You— you can go . . ."

"And what about them?" Koté interrupted.

"They," said the old man quickly, "they will go with

Metodija to that tiny field of mine to dig potatoes. As soon as I'm ready I'll take the letter of permission to them."

Koté bit his lip, put his hands on the table, and raised himself up to go. He forced himself to get up without saying a word. He only murmured, "As you say . . ."

"As it should be, Koté. As it should be," said the mayor, getting up after him. "Don't you worry as long as I'm the mayor here. You protect me and I'll protect you.

They all walked together into the courtyard. Then the mayor moved closer to them. He slowly eased himself among them and spoke with a confidential tone, "Let's keep it a secret, but I can also write a letter of permission saying that they're Serbs. I'll explain that's why I've let them go and . . ."

The three of them looked at him in astonishment, but they didn't understand. After a short pause, the mayor continued, "If they encounter Greeks, they'll produce the Greek letter; if they encounter Serbs, the Serbian one."

All three men stared at him in admiration and pleasure.

"Write, then. Don't talk any more," Koté said.

"I know," said the mayor, scratching behind his ear, "but the second letter is against the law."

"Who cares about the law?" asked Koté. "These men need to be saved."

"I know," said the mayor, "but just imagine if both letters were found. They'll get what's coming to them, but there's no hope for me, either."

Once again the three relatives exchanged glances.

"Any suggestions?" asked Koté after a time.

"Well," said the mayor, "if they have a gold piece, that would do nicely. But if they don't, there's nothing we can do. Over there," he directed his remarks to the cousins as he pointed in the direction of the fence, "on the other side of the river, toward the little fields in the valley, you can see Metodija in the field. The sooner you go, the sooner I'll bring you the notes."

The cousins looked at Koté. "Off you go," said Koté. "Go; go," said the mayor. "Metodija has already taken hoes for you."

Like unharnessed cattle, the cousins set off toward the gate. They bumped into each other, still confused. Then the mayor took hold of Koté's arm and led him toward the gate. "Don't you worry, Koté," he said. "If they've anything to hide, don't feel sorry for them. If they haven't, forget it. I hope they're lucky. No need for you to go to any expense." He almost pushed Koté out of the gate. "Go in peace. Regards to your family. Remember our talk. Don't worry at all. Remember what I said about your daughters. Another time I'll give you some more free advice . . ."

Koté walked down the path, feeling uneasy about what was behind him. He felt as if he were walking away from a snarling dog. "This one," he said to himself, "will reach the top. Nobody in these parts will ever complain of the Greeks. Everybody will be satisfied."

Srbin and Shishman had to work hard for the Greek mayor. It was fall already, when the harvest time is at its end. The chores were not strenuous, but there were many of them. Beans needed to be picked, corn had to be taken from the fields, cornstalks had to be cut and bundled and stacked in the fields. Potatoes had to be dug. The mayor had many fields, but not enough people to work them. Srbin and Shishman had come to him at just the right time. He kept them in his web with the letters of permission he had promised to give to them. In the evenings, when they had returned from the fields, and every morning before they went out, the cousins asked him, "Have you finished the letters? Do them today, if you can," they pleaded.

The mayor encouraged them. "Don't worry, lads," he would say, "you are in honest hands. Because of Koté, if for nothing else, I'll do everything I can for you. Do you understand? I have great plans for his daughters when the Greeks come to stay. My plans will be advantageous for you, too. Didn't you see written in the book that you from Breznitsa are Greeks? You'll need me, lads. You'll need me a lot. You'll see. I'll need you too. That's why, by day and night, I torture my head with those letters of yours. But writing is hard. You make a mistake with a comma, and someone's head will roll. If a fly shits on a word, the whole letter means something else. That's why you should just work and not interfere with my job."

Fortunately it started to rain heavily and cold weather set in. Because of the bad weather, and the fact they could no longer work, the mayor found it too expensive to feed the cousins. So he wrote the letters and let them go. Before they set off, they went to see their Uncle Koté. Koté advised them not to walk on the main road along the lake, but to climb high over the mountain. In this case they would probably have to walk two days before they reached Breznitsa, but it was a safer route. He filled their bags with bread, onions, and peppers, and gave them a bit of advice. "Whatever you do, never enter a village. The Greeks have their spies everywhere and you'll be reported. Also, try not to meet people. It doesn't matter whether you know them or not. Now is the worst time. You have just a short way to go. You have been lucky until now—somehow. But be aware that the last trap is the worst."

Luckily, it wasn't raining when they set off. The clouds were heavy and low, and the tops of the mountains were in fog. The cousins climbed up as they had been advised, first following the river. When they reached the highest part of the mountain, they would turn toward Breznitsa.

They were someplace high in the mountains, in a forest of large, old beech trees, when it started to rain. First it began to sprinkle, and then to rain more heavily. The cousins went under a huge beech tree, and waited there for the rain to stop. After about an hour, they continued their journey. Although it was no longer raining, they were up so high that they entered the fog. They could see so little, they were afraid they would miss the turn to Breznitsa. Although they didn't know where they were, they knew when they crossed over the top. They came out of the fog and entered another forest, this one filled with evergreens. As they walked through the forest, they heard a frightening roar. They stopped to listen, until they realized that the noise came from a river that had been flooded by the rain.

They continued walking. Then it started to rain again and to become dark. They decided to spend the night beside a large rock. They wanted to start a fire so they could get warm, but they didn't dare because they might be seen. It rained harder and harder. The roar of the river and the steady sound of the rain were so strong that the cousins felt they had been cornered. They slept for a while; then they woke up feeling cold. At one point in the night, the roar stopped and a dead silence filled the forest. Something had changed, but they didn't see until dawn that it was snowing.

Bewildered, they looked at the clean whiteness before them and wondered what they should do. "We must really be high in the mountains," said Srbin.

"Why do you think so?" asked Shishman.

"It's early for snow. At this time of year it snows only very high in the mountains."

"Yesterday we walked a long way down the mountain."

"Mountains are tricky if you're not familiar with them."

"We could get lost," said Shishman.

"We won't get lost. We will get ourselves on the right path. Let's go before we freeze."

"But where should we go?"

"Down," said Srbin.

"I can't hear the roar of the river."

"I can't either," said Srbin. "Anyway, we'll head down until we reach the river. When we get to it, we'll continue downward, following the river. If it's our river, we'll recognize it."

"But what if it isn't?"

"If it isn't, then it means we are on the same side as Lerin."

"Or Bitola."

"It can't be Bitola," said Srbin. "If we had gone in the direction of Bitola, we would have come to the trenches along the front."

They continued walking carefully in the thin layer of fresh snow, which was already melting. As they talked, they slowly warmed up. The fog became thicker and the snow gradually disappeared.

They came to a valley and climbed up a little hill, intending to walk along it. But suddenly they didn't know which side of the hill they should walk along. Srbin found himself confused and a bit frightened. He thought that they were probably lost, but then he reminded himself that the steep side of the mountain should be on their left. Since it was, they turned to the right. They walked for a long time, but there was no path. They didn't seem to arrive anywhere.

After they had walked for several hours, Shishman

said, "Cousin, it's strange, but I am hungry before we have arrived anyplace familiar."

Srbin stopped. "Yes," he said, "it is strange. I am hungry too. It's time for lunch."

"Perhaps it is because we are tired," said Shishman.

"It could be anything," said Srbin. "Let's have lunch and then see what will happen. We'll think better on a full stomach."

They sat on the root of a large old beech and opened their bags. Both of them ate without talking. While they were eating, the fog lifted and the sun shone faintly.

"Let's walk some more," said Srbin. "We'll try to get someplace. I don't know what happened!"

"We're lost, for sure," said Shishman.

"I don't know," said Srbin, as he started to walk.

They continued walking. After more than an hour they were still nowhere familiar.

"Dear God!" Shishman kept repeating. "I don't know . . . ." Then he stopped, bewildered. "Look!" he said to Srbin.

Srbin looked at him and turned his head to where Shishman pointed. Then he saw something familiar. "We are at the same place where we ate our lunch." He went straight to the place under the beech tree. It was exactly the same place. "We have been circling around the hill," said Srbin.

"Like horses circling a field," said Shishman.

They were embarrassed, but at the same time they were glad to know what they had been doing.

Then Srbin started to go straight down the mountain. "When we come to a valley, let's walk downward along the valley. I know that's right," said Srbin.

"We should be careful, cousin," said Shishman.

They came to a stream and started to walk downward along it. Soon the area began to look familiar. After a time, Srbin stopped, turned toward Shishman, and looked him straight in the eyes. For a few minutes they stared at each other.

"We are in the Rupa!" said Shishman.

"We're home!" said Srbin.

"Now I'll put the pebble in the canteen," said Shishman.

"No," said Srbin, without knowing why.

Shishman was disappointed and they continued in silence. Further on, below a meadow, they sat down on a tree trunk to rest. The sun shone through the clouds from time to time, first one place and then another. Still, it looked as if it might rain again.

Suddenly they heard something unusual. They stood up and looked at each other. They didn't have time to think about it. Srbin silently turned in the direction of the meadow and went into the bushes. Shishman followed him.

They walked slowly, on their tiptoes, side by side. They went around a big bush and saw two bears chasing each other in the middle of the meadow. Srbin and Shishman smiled at each other. One of the bears chased the other, and then they entered the forest, one following the other. Srbin and Shishman looked after them.

"Like kids, aren't they?" Shishman said. "They've gone to look for their mothers."

"So the wheel turns," said Srbin. "Children search for their mothers, and fathers search for their children."

From the meadow on the Vojnik, Srbin and Shishman saw Breznitsa down in the valley beneath them. They stopped and took a deep breath. The rain clouds hung low and the wind blew gusts of frost crystals about the village, so that the houses looked as if they were in a whirlpool without a bottom. To the cousins, it all seemed inaccessible.

"We're here!" said Shishman.

"Perhaps," said Srbin.

They went straight down the hill. They could hardly keep themselves on their feet, even though they were careful to work their heels into the ground diagonally, digging in as deep as they could so they wouldn't be toppled by the steepness. Shishman was in front. Srbin, behind him, had to be careful not to rush into his cousin, to push him down, and then to fly over him. They would tumble down like rocks. Once Srbin's foot deceived him, but he grabbed hold of a root and managed to maintain his balance.

Shishman felt Srbin push against him and hurried to take a new step. But his foot slipped as well. Unable to stop himself, he ran downhill, pulled by his own weight. As stocky as he was, he was suddenly left with no other choice. He ran down the hill, zigzagging like a wild goat. Far down, at the edge of a ravine overgrown with beech, he managed to grab hold of a tree trunk. He spun around it with his free arm lifted. His eyes were fixed above him, on Srbin. At that moment, Srbin let go of the branch he was holding and rushed down the hill. Shishman experienced both fear and joy as he watched his cousin fly. It seemed his speed would tear the clothes off his body. In front of the beech tree where Shishman waited, the ground was slightly flat. Srbin managed to catch hold of the tree opposite him.

Laughing, they looked at one another and then became aware that it was now raining. They decided to hurry. Entering the woods above the next ravine, they began to walk down the lumberjacks' path. They didn't feel the rain on their skin, but they could hear its tapping on the leaves. They felt as if they were walking beside a rising river. The weather made them feel drugged, even exalted. Shishman felt such pleasure as they were walking down the wide path that he picked up a pebble and put it in his canteen. The rattling of the pebble echoed in Shishman's ears like an accompaniment to the music of the rain on the leaves in the woods around them.

"Can you hear anything?" Shishman asked Srbin. "I put the pebble in."

"Good," said Srbin.

"But without asking you," said Shishman.

"Good," said Srbin. "It's different now."

They turned uphill onto a road that passed by the little church at St. Archangel. The rain became heavier, chillier. The breeze blew from time to time and drove the fat rain drops straight into their faces. Before they even reached the little church, the rain had drenched their hats and the water had run through their hair onto their necks. The rain was getting heavier and heavier, as it usually does before snow. They hurried as fast as they could, but resisted the temptation to run.

Just past the church, Shishman stopped—suddenly, as if he had been stuck to the spot. Puzzled, Srbin looked at him. Shishman seemed terrified.

"We didn't cross ourselves," Shishman said breathlessly.

They turned around quickly and fixed their eyes on the wall of the church. Their heads buried in their shoulders, they crossed themselves quickly. Then they resumed their journey. From the road they saw Alexso Dzvezdin's hayloft and debated for a moment whether to take shelter under it, but they decided there was no point in lingering. They were already drenched to their skins and were only a few steps from home. So they continued walking. The rain began to fall even more heavily. Fog surrounded them, and the rain settled into an even downpour. They walked along steadily, hurrying, of course, but without running. After a time they came to a road that descended in a straight line to the bridge that led into the village. Empty, harvested fields stood on both sides. Because the land was rocky, the fields were surrounded by high stone walls that made them look like boxes, and the road was also lined with stone walls on both sides. Nobody was in sight. The cornstalks that Trajan Petreski stored on a branch of a big walnut tree by the road looked like a monster trapped in the tree.

As they continued their walk down the road, they thought they would swerve before the bridge and walk up the river for a way. Then they would hide in German's mill until someone from the village would come along and tell them whether the village was safe. They walked shoulder to shoulder, staggering and bumping into one another. They kept tripping over stones that turned over and rolled, rattling like walnuts. Suddenly, they stopped. Someone seemed to have said something, and he seemed to be speaking to them.

They had understood what he had said. It was Serbian. The words expressed wonder about their destination in such bad weather. The cousins stood still, hardly breathing. Slowly, very slowly, they turned their heads. Then they turned to each other and exchanged disbelieving glances. In each other's eyes they saw stark fear. Each felt a weakness in his knees. In mute agreement, they both turned their heads back and looked over the wall beneath a bundle of cornstalks. No one was there. They glanced at one another again, and checked for a second time. As they started to resume their journey more quietly, they noticed that the rain had slowed down and the air had cleared—so it was easier to breathe.

They watched each other, carefully taking one step forward, slowly, then another, and another. On the third step, the pebble in Shishman's canteen rattled as if it had been stung by a bee. They both stopped, and Shishman covered the canteen with his large hand as if to silence it. But in the excitement, Shishman moved, and the pebble rattled again. The cousins found themselves trapped by the pebble. Shishman thrust out his hip and the two men looked at the canteen as if it were a sparrow they had caught. Srbin held the canteen with great care. As he began to turn it slowly so the pebble would slide out, somebody behind the wall spoke in loud, clear Serbian. "What are you snooping around here for, damn you?"

Both Shishman's hip and Srbin's hands began to tremble, and the pebble rattled again. They had no time to look back. Srbin pulled himself together, and with an ultimate effort slowly turned the canteen upside down. The pebble slid out. It fell into a puddle made by a horseshoe print, so it made no sound.

They lifted their eyes and saw two Serbian soldiers coming toward them from behind the wall. Their round faces peeked out from under their flattened caps. Srbin fixed his gaze on one of them and unconsciously opened his mouth. He turned cold when he saw the taller one staring and heard him say something reflecting surprise. The soldier had recognized him. Leaning his rifle against the wall, the soldier eagerly gripped the stones at the top of the wall with both hands and jumped over. Then he slung the rifle back on his shoulder. He fixed his eyes on Srbin and moved quickly, as if he were afraid that the cousins would suddenly be swallowed by the earth. He walked over to the cousins and stood before them.

"Hey, you!" he said slowly, as if he were about to faint from astonishment. "Didn't I recruit you both at Vlasotintsa? You are those brothers or cousins who were going abroad to work, aren't you? You put on the uniforms without protesting and pretended you were going to look for the Serbian army. Well, then, screw both of you, as well as your sisters, your grandmothers, and all the women in your family down to a baby of half a kilo! How come you're here at home, when not a soul from the Serbian army has been released yet?"

The cousins stood silent. They felt as if they were becoming smaller and smaller, so small they might even melt away. Both of them recognized the intruder. He was the one who had caught them at Vlasotintsa, when they were on their way to earn money in Wallachia at the beginning of the war. What the devil brought him here? And at the end of their journey! He knew them so well—like his own pocket. All they needed now was to be identified as Bulgarian soldiers. And they carried letters from the mayor who represented the Greeks in Livadje.

The soldier demanded no answers. He only looked at them as if they were tables filled with rich food. He was sure that these chickens were full of eggs. Every Serbian soldier in Macedonia knew very well that in spite of all the poverty in the area, there were pearls in the oyster shells. He turned to the other soldier, who still stood behind the wall, under the tree that held the cornstalks. "Come out, Miladin! Come here, come!" he said in slow delight. "Come and see a wonder among wonders!"

Miladin climbed the wall and came nearer. Keeping an eye on the cousins, the first soldier spoke again to Miladin. "Come, Miladin, take the canteen away from the one who looks like an ox. I'm dying to see it."

Miladin remained indifferent, but he obeyed. Shishman handed over the canteen. The first soldier looked at the canteen from every angle. Suddenly angry, he threw it over the wall into the field. He spoke through clenched teeth, "Bulgarian! That's what I thought."

Then he looked again at Shishman. He focused his eyes on him and looked him up and down, from his head to his toes. "Ha!" he said, and took his rifle off his shoulder. He handed it to Miladin to hold for a while and went toward Shishman. He was in high spirits as he lifted the drenched cap off Shishman's head. "If I could only find an empty shoe polish tin in your pocket, I'd feel much better, you know," he said.

The soldier squatted before Shishman, as if he were following a ritual. He put his hands on Shishman's hips and began to feel up and down all over his wide homespun trousers. He began at the waist and slowly felt down the trousers, all the way to Shishman's knees. As he did so, he said to his companion, "Just you watch, Miladin. I read him like an open book! You see how big the bugger is, but he goes nowhere without an empty shoe polish tin. When he's in the mood, he puts a pebble in it so it will rattle. So he can be taken for a fool. And as for this other one, who looks like a baby goat, the sound is like music. Just you watch." He spoke, but as yet he could find nothing. Perhaps the problem was the size of the pants and the thickness of the patched homespun cloth. The soldier stood up and slipped his hand into Shishman's deep front pocket. Since the pockets needed darning, his hand slipped through the pocket hole as far as his elbow.

Then, suddenly, something happened. The soldier's hand stopped moving inside the pants and his face became thoughtful. A moment later he smiled happily. He raised his eyes and looked at Srbin. Still smiling, but now mockingly, he withdrew his hand from Shishman's trousers as if nothing had happened. Then he stood straight before the cousins. He began to rub the palms of his hands together, licking his lips and saying, "So! And I, the fool, was almost angry with you! You are like that duck in the fairy tale that was left on a bridge by a rich man for me to find. Only unlike the poor man in the story, I think I am smart enough to keep what I find." He half-turned to Miladin and waved his hand at him. Then he spat in the palm of his hand, rubbed his hands together, and put his hands on his hips. In an imperious voice he commanded the cousins: "Now, boys: DOWN WITH YOUR PANTS!"

The cousins could feel the resistance pulsing through their veins, but their eyes expressed bewilderment. They tensed themselves, like mice about to be attacked by a cat. Then, realizing their helplessness, they went limp. They looked at one another helplessly. Both of them were ready to cry.

"You're wasting your time," the soldier said. Without turning, he stretched his arms toward Miladin. "Miladin," he said, "pass me the rifle, please." He slowly took the rifle, loaded it and spoke very slowly. "I'll count to three." He pressed his elbow against the butt of the rifle. "One," he said and waited a little.

The cousins were weeping openly now. They looked like deer pleading for their lives. The soldier with the rifle wasn't in a hurry.

"Two," he said after a while.

The cousins debated. They looked at each other once again, as if they were about to separate for a long time. Srbin was the first to reach for his belt. Shishman followed. Again they looked at each other with sympathy and they cried silently, without voices, like children. When they touched their belt buckles, they stopped, in futile hope that something would change. Then the soldier shouted at them impatiently, "Unbuckle your belts!"

Even after the cousins had unbuckled their belts, they still held their trousers up with their hands. They pressed their wrists against their stomachs and stooped in a protective posture. The trousers were so bulky and full that they had dropped below their buttocks. Now they were held up only by an instinctive resistance against humiliation.

"Let them drop!" the soldier shouted angrily and impatiently.

Their trousers dropped below their knees. The soldier's face lit up with a delighted smile. He spoke calmly to Miladin. "And now, Miladin, take your knife and cut the hems of their undershirts. You'll see what golden trinkets we'll find for our wives."

Miladin obeyed, although he wasn't quite sure what was going on. He went toward them with the knife clenched in his hand and grabbed the hem of Srbin's undershirt first. With his fingers he felt the coins sewn in the hem and then turned to his companion, his teeth glittering with joy.

"Don't think," the soldier said to him. "Work! You are digging for gold!"

Quickly and nervously, Miladin began to rip rather than cut. He didn't notice that Shishman cried out in pain when the knife stabbed his thigh. Miladin concentrated his gaze on the gold coins that were falling from the hem of the undershirt onto the ground. When the coins from the undershirts of both cousins were in his hands, he pressed them tightly against his heart. Then he drew back, stumbling over the stones in the road, turning away, as if from sin. His companion aimed the rifle between them and spoke. "Now get lost. All is fair and square. You paid for your desertion and we have been rewarded for letting you go. Not a word to a soul if you think well of your families and yourselves. Understand? Come, now! Pull up your trousers—spare me the sight. Pull them up, I say! Now beat it! Get lost! Shoooooooo. Do you hear?" He stamped his foot, threatening them as if they were chickens.

The cousins turned to face one another. With their heads cocked to one side, each looked to the other. Then they turned around until their opposite shoulders touched. They kept their backs to the soldiers and began to walk down the road. They leaned tightly against each other, as they had done when they were boys.

The soldiers stood watching them go toward the village and disappear around the bend in the road. As they turned to the right, the soldiers saw their wet clothes steaming on their backs, drying after the rain.

The weather was clearing. Between the clouds the sky was intensely blue.

7 8/23/88

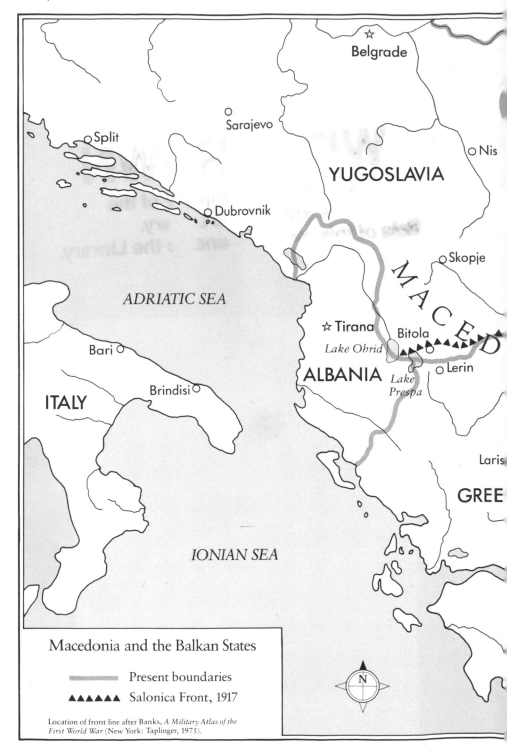

Belgrade

Sarajevo

Split

Nis

YUGOSLAVIA

Dubrovnik

Skopje

ADRIATIC SEA

M A C E D

Tirana
Bitola

Lake Ohrid

Bari

ALBANIA
*Lake
Prespa*

Lerin

Brindisi

ITALY

Laris

GREE

IONIAN SEA

Macedonia and the Balkan States

━━━ Present boundaries

▲▲▲▲▲▲ Salonica Front, 1917

N

Location of front line after Banks, *A Military Atlas of the
First World War* (New York: Taplinger, 1975).